T

St. Helens Libraries

Please return / renew this item by the last date shown.
Books may also be renewed by phone and Internet.
Telephone – (01744) 676954 or 677822
Email – centrallibrary@sthelens.gov.uk
Online – http://eps.sthelens.gov.uk/rooms

LiP -

THE ROYAL FLUSH MURDERS

Superintendent Budd is called in by the local police of Long Millford to investigate the strange murder of John Brockwell, impaled to the trunk of a tree with a pitchfork. Pinned to the lapel of the dead man's jacket is a playing card: the ten of diamonds. What is the meaning of this sign left on the body? Who hates the unpleasant Brockwell family so intensely, and why?

GERALD VERNER

◆

THE ROYAL FLUSH MURDERS

Complete and Unabridged

LINFORD
Leicester

First published in Great Britain

First Linford Edition
published 2014

A catalogue record for this book is available
from the British Library.

ISBN 978–1–4448–1907–6

Published by
F. A. Thorpe (Publishing)
Anstey, Leicestershire

Set by Words & Graphics Ltd.
Anstey, Leicestershire
Printed and bound in Great Britain by
T. J. International Ltd., Padstow, Cornwall

This book is printed on acid-free paper

For
My Wife
With Love

Part One

The Ten of Diamonds

1

In company with the rest of the executives at Scotland Yard, Superintendent Robert Budd looked askance at any crime that had about it the elements of what he called, disparagingly, 'story-book stuff.' Murder in real life was usually sordid, with none of the trimmings so beloved of the sensational novelist. A man killed his wife in a fit of drunken temper, or from jealousy, or because he wanted to marry another woman, and he did it in the crudest and most stupid manner. There was no mystery about it. No 'impossible' crimes behind sealed doors with long lists of 'suspects,' each of whom had the strongest possible motive and, therefore, had nothing whatever to do with it at all. In real life the obvious people were usually the right ones and all the police had to do was to collect sufficient evidence against them to ensure a conviction when they were brought to trial. Sometimes this was difficult, but not very often, and the toughest case usually yielded to routine; that combination of diligent research and questioning which Scotland Yard has brought to a fine art. There was no romance in it; no thrills; no dramatic dénouements. Just a plain, hard job of work, like laying bricks or digging coal.

When, therefore, Mr. Budd read in his newspaper of the murder at Long Millford with its unusual features, he snorted disparagingly and muttered 'hokum' under his breath. The crime was, certainly, sufficiently out of the ordinary run of such things to place it in a category of its own. The youngest son of a Mr. Henry Brockwell had been found by a forester, on his way to work, impaled to the trunk of a tree with a pitchfork. The prongs had passed right through his chest, one of them piercing the heart, and the medical evidence at the inquest testified that death must have been instantaneous. The curious feature, which the newspapers had seized upon with avidity, was the fact that pinned to the lapel of the dead man's

4

jacket was a playing-card — the ten of diamonds. It was this, and the unusual method of the murder, which lifted the crime out of the commonplace and caused the press to give it so much prominence.

Mr. Budd, despite his openly expressed disapproval, was sufficiently interested to follow the investigation by the local police, or as much of it as he could glean from the newspapers, and to make several caustic comments when at the expiration of three weeks no arrest had been made and the police admitted that they were without a single clue that was likely to lead to the identity of the murderer. It seemed incredible that they had been unable to discover anything at all. The very strangeness of the crime should have made its solution easier. The weapon was unusual. The playing-card pinned to the coat — real 'story-book stuff', this — was even more unusual. Surely from all these things the local police should have been able to find some reason — some motive — that would indicate who was responsible for the murder? But apparently they hadn't, or else they were keeping it very much to themselves. Perhaps that was it.

Mr. Budd, sitting in the chair behind his desk in his cheerless little office at Scotland Yard, cogitated drowsily over the matter, his eyes closed and his hands clasped loosely over his capacious stomach. The soft buzzing of the house telephone roused him, just as he was on the point of falling into a doze, and he reached out and picked up the receiver.

'Hullo?' he said, in his husky rumble. 'Oh, yes, sir. Now? Yes, sir, I'll come at once.'

He jammed the receiver back on its rack and hoisted himself with difficulty out of the tight embrace of the chair. As he went ponderously over to the door, it opened to admit the lean and lanky form of Sergeant Leek.

'Hullo,' said the sergeant. 'Where are you goin'?'

'Why don't you knock instead of comin' bargin' in like that?' demanded Mr. Budd severely. 'I've told you about it over an' over again . . .'

'I always forget,' murmured Leek. 'Where are you goin'?'

'To see the Assistant Commissioner,' said the big man.

'Oh!' said Leek. 'What does 'e want?'

'How do I know until I've seen 'im?' snarled Mr. Budd. 'Don't stand there blockin' up the doorway. I'm in a hurry . . . '

The melancholy sergeant stepped aside with a sigh, and Mr. Budd left the office and went with portly dignity in search of the Assistant Commissioner.

Colonel Blair, neat and trim as usual, was sitting behind his huge desk studying the contents of a folder when the big superintendent came in.

'Sit down, Budd,' he said, nodding towards a chair in front of the desk. 'Do you know anything about this business at Long Millford?'

Mr. Budd's drooping eyelids shot upwards. So *that* was it, was it? The 'locals' had asked for help.

'Only what I've read in the newspapers, sir,' he answered heavily, as he perched himself gingerly on the chair.

'Then you know as much, or as little, as I do,' grunted the Assistant Commissioner. 'The local police have made no headway at all, and the Chief Constable, under pressure from the dead man's father, has asked for our help. I'm sending you down and you'd better take Sergeant Leek with you. Superintendent Tidworthy is in charge of the case and he'll give you all the facts, or as many as he knows, when you get there. Long Millford is a tiny place, tucked away in the Hampshire downs, and miles away from anywhere. The nearest town is Bedlington and you're meeting Tidworthy there at the police station. The Chief Constable, Major Toppington, will be there, too. There's a train from Waterloo which gets to Bedlington at three-forty-five and I've told them that you'll be there at four o'clock . . .'

'I'd rather go in my car, sir,' interrupted Mr. Budd.

'Just as you like,' said Colonel Blair, wondering privately how much longer it was going to be before that ancient machine fell to pieces. 'But you *must* reach there by four o'clock. I understand that they're holding a conference.' He frowned, leaned back in his chair and passed a hand over his smooth, grey hair. 'It's a queer business, altogether,' he went on, staring at the ceiling. 'I can't give you any more details than you've already got from the newspapers, but no doubt Superintendent Tidworthy will be able to amplify those. If he can't — well, I'm sure you'll be able to unearth something on your own account. You've got a good record, Budd, and I'm giving you this case with perfect confidence . . . '

'Thank you, sir,' murmured Mr. Budd, hoping that his confidence would be justified.

'I'm sure you'll find out the truth,' continued the Assistant Commissioner, 'though, of course, the fact that it is over three weeks since the murder took place is going to make it more difficult.' He gave an irritable twist to his shoulders. 'If only these people would call us in at once instead of waiting until they've failed to get results themselves. However, I suppose they never will and we've just got to make the best of it.'

'Yes, sir,' said Mr. Budd.

'You'd better arrange to stay in the

district if you think it necessary,' said
Colonel Blair, and then he added abruptly:
'Well, I think that's all. Good luck.'

'Thank you, sir,' said Mr. Budd, and
he got ponderously to his feet. He would
need a lot of good luck, he thought
gloomily, as he made his way back to his
own room. Any clues there might have
been were probably destroyed by now
. . . Well, he could only do his best . . .

2

The noisy contraption which Mr. Budd referred to as his car, by some species of miracle that defied all the laws of mechanics, transported its portly owner and the melancholy Sergeant Leek from London to Bedlington without mishap and brought them to a squeaky stop in front of the police station at precisely a quarter to four.

'Well, here we are,' remarked the big man, wearily squeezing himself from behind the wheel and stepping down on to the pavement. 'Let's go an' see what they've got in store for us.'

He went into the police station, followed by the lugubrious Leek, and introduced himself to the desk-sergeant.

'The Sooper's expectin' you, sir,' said that grizzled man. ''E's in 'is office with Major Toppington.' He got down from behind his desk and led the way over to a closed door opening off the charge-room.

On this he tapped. A gruff voice growled an invitation to 'come in' and the desk-sergeant opened the door.

'Sup'ntendent Budd from Scotland Yard, sir,' he announced, importantly, and he stood aside for Mr. Budd and Sergeant Leek to go in.

The small room contained three people. Behind a flat-topped desk sat a thin man with an almost completely bald head and a straggling ginger-grey moustache. By the fireplace, one arm resting on the mantelshelf, stood a short, plump little man with a round face and horn-rimmed spectacles that were so large that they gave him a queer, blank, owlish expression. The third man was standing by the window and turned quickly as he heard the desk-sergeant's announcement. He was thick-set with a face that looked as though it had been hewn out of wood with a blunt axe, and the hewer had not been very particular as to what sort of a job he made of it.

The man behind the desk stood up as they came in.

'You're very punctual, Superintendent,'

he said, in a broad Hampshire dialect. 'My name's Tidworthy. This is the Chief Constable, Major Toppington' — he indicated the man by the fireplace — 'and that is Sergeant Mackleberry . . . '

Mr. Budd acknowledged the introductions and introduced Leek.

'Perhaps you'd like a cup of tea after your journey, Superintendent?' suggested the Chief Constable, pleasantly. 'We might all have one, don't you think, Tidworthy?'

'Yes, sir.' The thin man turned to the sergeant. 'Go along to the canteen, Mackleberry, will you, and bring in a tray.'

The sergeant nodded shortly and went out.

'Sit down, Superintendent,' said the Chief Constable, indicating a vacant chair in front of the desk. 'I'm afraid you'll have to sit on the window ledge, Sergeant. There isn't very much room in this place . . . '

'What about you, sir?' asked Mr. Budd.

'Don't worry about me,' answered Major Toppington. 'I'd rather stand. I prefer standing.'

A little gingerly, for the chair did not look overly substantial, Mr. Budd lowered his massive bulk down onto it. It creaked a little but, to his relief, stood up under the strain. The Chief Constable resumed his original position by the fireplace, and Tidworthy sat down again behind his desk.

Sergeant Mackleberry came in with five large cups of steaming tea on a tray, which he handed round in stolid silence.

'Now,' said Major Toppington, after a preliminary gulp from his cup. 'Let's get to business, shall we? What do you know about this very queer affair, Superintendent?'

'Nuthin', sir,' replied Mr. Budd. The tea was horrible — strong and over-sweetened. 'Nuthin' except what I've read in the newspapers.'

'Then I think the best thing would be for Tidworthy to give you a brief résumé of the facts, don't you?' suggested the Chief Constable. 'You can then ask any questions that occur to you and we'll answer them if we can . . .'

Mr. Budd agreed that this was a very good suggestion and Superintendent Tidworthy produced a black-covered book, cleared his throat, and began:

'The murder was discovered on the morning of May the fifth,' he said. 'A forester named Abel Garth, on his way to lop some dangerous trees on the estate of Sir Oswald Pipp-Parkington, took a short cut through Cooper's Spinney. There's a big elm tree in the middle of the spinney an' he saw something 'uddled against the trunk. What it was he couldn't make out at first, but when 'e got closer he found that it was young John Brockwell . . . '

'Who was Brockwell?' interposed Mr. Budd, partially opening his eyes.

'The youngest son of Henry Brockwell, who lives at the Croft on the outskirts o' Long Millford,' answered Tidworthy. 'I'll tell you all about the Brockwells later on. As I was sayin', Garth saw that it was John Brockwell an' that he was dead. He'd been fixed to the trunk of the elm tree by the prongs of a pitchfork which 'ad gone clean through his chest, and the whole of the front of him was smothered in blood. Garth gave the alarm and about an hour after he'd made the discovery — that is, round about nine-thirty — me

15

an' Sergeant Mackleberry were on the spot. Doctor Middlesham, the local doctor, had already examined the body an' given his opinion, and our own police surgeon, Doctor Wakefield, confirmed all that 'e said. Death had taken place between one-thirty and three o'clock that morning and must have been instantaneous. One prong of the pitchfork had been driven right through the heart. The weapon must have been used with great force, because after passing through the body it was embedded nearly two inches in the tree trunk . . .'

'Um,' murmured Mr. Budd, his eyes fixed dreamily on the stained ceiling. 'Interestin' — interestin' an' peculiar. How did the murderer get this feller to stand quietly up against the tree while he lunged at him with the pitchfork?'

'That's one of the things that's been puzzlin' me,' said Tidworthy. 'Brockwell must have had some warning of what he was going to do, or so you'd think, wouldn't you? A pitchfork ain't like a knife or a pistol. You couldn't conceal it, could you? You'd 'ave thought that

Brockwell would have put up some sort of a fight . . . '

'There wasn't any sign of a struggle?' asked the big man.

Superintendent Tidworthy shook his head.

'No,' he answered, 'an' it was soft ground round that tree, too. If there'd been anything of the sort it couldn't have failed to leave traces.'

'Very peculiar,' remarked Mr. Budd, thoughtfully. 'Very peculiar indeed. 'Ow old was this feller, John Brockwell?'

'Not quite twenty-one,' said Tidworthy, looking a little surprised at the question.

'Not quite twenty-one, eh?' repeated Mr. Budd. ''Ave you any idea what he was doin' in this place, Cooper's Spinney, at one-thirty in the mornin'?'

'No.' The local superintendent shook his head. 'I realized the importance of that, an' we've done all we could to find out, but with no luck . . . '

'It's my idea,' put in Major Toppington, 'that there's a woman mixed up in this somewhere, though we haven't been able to find her . . . '

'Meanin' that Brockwell may have gone to Cooper's Spinney to keep an appointment with some girl or other?' said Mr. Budd. 'Well, sir, there may be somethin' in that. In which case it 'ud seem that jealousy might be at the bottom of it?'

'We've been over all that,' said Tidworthy, 'and we can't discover anything at all to confirm such a theory. And it doesn't explain the queerest thing of all — the playing-card that was pinned to the dead man's coat . . . '

'Ah, yes,' said Mr. Budd, his drooping eyelids shooting up like suddenly released spring shutters. 'The playin'-card. The ten of diamonds, wasn't it?'

'Yes.' Tidworthy nodded. 'I've got it here.' He opened a drawer in his desk and brought out an envelope. From it he carefully extracted a stained and crumpled card.

'You can handle it without worrying,' he said. 'We've had it tested for fingerprints and there were none.'

'None at all?' said Mr. Budd, with interest.

'Not a single one,' declared the local

superintendent. 'Nor on the handle of the pitchfork.'

'H'm, that means the murderer wore gloves,' said Mr. Budd, taking the card between a fat thumb and finger, 'which would appear to suggest that the crime was planned carefully. Did you find out where the pitchfork came from?'

'Yes, but it didn't help us at all,' answered Tidworthy. 'It was stolen from Antrim's farm two days before the murder.'

Mr. Budd made no comment. He was peering at the card he held in his hand. It was rather a gruesome-looking object, for the dead man's blood had dried on it in dark streaks, partially obliterating the diamond-shaped pips. It was not a new card, but old and crumpled. Mr. Budd looked at the back. The design was ordinary — a geometrical pattern in deep blue. It might have come from any one of thousands of packs. The big man had seen and handled hundreds of such cards. After a long scrutiny he passed it back to Tidworthy.

'I s'pose it's struck you that this feller

may be a lunatic?' he said, rubbing his fleshy chin. 'The killer, I mean.'

'Naturally we have considered that possibility,' said Major Toppington. 'But it hasn't got us anywhere. Whether he is a lunatic or not, we haven't been able to find him, and that's what matters.'

Mr. Budd started to yawn, recollected that it might look a little rude, and checked himself.

'An' these are all the facts, eh?' he said.

Superintendent Tidworthy nodded.

'Every blessed one of 'em,' he answered, gloomily. 'We've worked like slaves over this, Superintendent, and we've found out practically nothing more than when we started.'

'It's up to you now,' said the Chief Constable, pleasantly.

'Thank you, sir,' murmured Mr. Budd, without any marked degree of enthusiasm. 'I'll do everythin' I can, but on the face of it it looks as though it was goin' ter be pretty difficult. All we've got to go on is this: A feller called John Brockwell was killed between the hours of one-thirty an' three in the mornin' in a place called

Cooper's Spinney by havin' a pitchfork stuck through 'im. An old playin'-card, the ten of diamonds, was pinned to 'is coat. There were no finger-prints either on the card or on the pitchfork, which was stolen from the farmyard of a Mr . . . what-was-the-name?'

'Antrim — Charles Antrim,' volunteered Tidworthy.

'An' that's all,' went on Mr. Budd. 'Not what you could call a superfluity o' clues, is it? What sort of a feller was this Brockwell?'

Superintendent Tidworthy looked at Major Toppington, as though mutely suggesting that *he* should answer that.

'Well . . . ' The Chief Constable pursed his lips and considered for a moment. 'Well, he wasn't a very nice — er — specimen,' he said, after a slight pause. 'None of the Brockwells are, for that matter. A very queer lot . . . '

'How d'you mean, sir, exactly?' inquired Mr. Budd.

'I think it would be better for you to find out for yourself,' replied Major Toppington. 'I don't want to put any

21

prejudices into your mind, and we hold rather strong views about the Brockwells in this district. Mr. Henry Brockwell expressed a wish to see you as soon as possible after your arrival, so I think it would be a good idea if, when we have finished here, we go over to Long Millford and pay him a visit.'

3

The village of Long Millford, although it is unmarked on any but the larger ordnance maps, is one of the few remaining unspoiled beauty-spots of rural England. It consists of one main street with half a dozen tiny shops, a handful of cottages, one or two fine old houses, a church, and a pub called The Peal o' Bells.

Mr. Budd's first sight of it on that May evening impressed him with its old-world, peaceful beauty. Here was a loveliness that man in his insane thirst for 'progress' was fast destroying. Here the air was sweet and clean, unsmirched by the sooty, sulphurous smoke of factory chimney, and the birds sang tunefully, their liquid notes undrowned by the strident roar and clatter of the machine. Here was man's original birthright which in his ignorance and blindness he was selling for a pottage of speed. Faster, faster! Quicker, quicker!

The brainless parrot-cry rose, shrilly discordant, all over the world, repeated and echoed by the whirling wheels and thrashing pistons. No time to think, no time to enjoy. Get there. Get back. Get somewhere else. Faster, faster! Quicker, quicker! Chain yourselves, you poor, witless, deluded creatures, to the mass of vibrating metal of your own creation and go hurtling forward in search of a brave new world, missing in your headlong rush all the joys and beauty that the old has to offer.

The sinking sun was sending long golden streaks of light athwart the narrow street as Mr. Budd drove his dilapidated car down it. The Croft, the house in which the Brockwells lived, was on the outskirts of Long Millford, and from Bedlington they had to pass through the village to reach it. They turned into a narrow lane, foaming and fragrant with hawthorn, and came eventually within sight of the house.

'God Almighty!' breathed Mr. Budd, involuntarily.

'That,' remarked Major Toppington,

bitterly, 'was once a lovely sixteenth-century manor house surrounded by some of the finest trees in the district. Now look at it!'

Mr. Budd looked aghast at the eyesore that confronted him.

'It . . . it's like a picture palace,' he said. 'You can almost imagine 'Super Cinema' sprawlin' across the front in neon lights . . . '

'That's what Brockwell did,' growled the Chief Constable, disgustedly, 'when he bought the place four years ago. He had all the trees cut down, pulled down the old house and erected this monstrosity in its place. Everybody in the neighbourhood raised an indignant protest, but it didn't do any good . . . '

'It must have cost a good bit o' money,' said the big man, as he sent the car slowly through the ornate entrance to the drive and along the smooth yellow gravel, bordered by very geometrical flower-beds which looked as though somebody had scattered a lot of jam tarts on a green baize cloth.

'Oh, there's no lack of money,' said

Major Toppington. 'Brockwell appears to be rolling in it . . . '

'How did 'e get it?' asked Mr. Budd.

'Timber,' answered the Chief Constable, shortly. 'He started as a lumberjack in Canada, I believe.'

Mr. Budd stopped the car in front of a very wide, shallow flight of marble steps that led up to a huge door of shiny black and chromium. Major Toppington sprang out with great agility and the stout man followed ponderously. They went up the steps and pressed a bell-push. Faintly from inside came a musical chime of tubular bells.

'Just like somethin' out of an American film,' murmured Mr. Budd. 'If Betty Grable answers the door in glorious Technicolor, I wouldn't be surprised . . . '

The person who did open the door, however, succeeded in achieving that which might have been denied to Miss Grable. He was a small, thin-faced man with scanty sandy hair, and Mr. Budd's sleepy eyes opened very wide when they saw him.

'Well, well,' he remarked. 'If it isn't

Tommy Custer. How did you get here, Tommy?'

The little man's surprise was obviously equal to his own. He made a valiant, if ineffectual, effort to hide it, however.

'I don't know what you mean,' he grunted. 'Mistaken me for someone else, ain't you, sir?'

Mr. Budd shook his head.

'How could I ever mistake you for anybody else, Tommy?' he answered, gently. 'Didn't I pull you in for pinchin' Lady Longfordham's jewels eight years ago . . . '

'Do you know this man?' broke in the Chief Constable, in astonishment.

'Very well indeed,' said Mr. Budd. 'Very well indeed, sir. How long 'ave you bin out, Tommy?'

The ferrety face of the man he called 'Tommy' set harshly and his small eyes blazed with suppressed fury.

'You leave me alone,' he snapped. 'I'm goin' straight now, I am. Earnin' an honest livin' . . . '

'As straight as a corkscrew,' said the big man, 'I'll bet you are. If they used you as a ruler ter draw a straight line it 'ud look like a map of the Alps. What are you doin' here, Tom?'

'Now see 'ere,' said Mr. Custer, belligerently. 'You've got no right ter talk to me like that. I've got a good job an' I'm doin' it to the best of me ability, see. I'm workin' as butler for Mr. Brockwell . . . '

'An' makin' quite a few pickin's, I'll be bound,' murmured Mr. Budd. 'You always was an opportunist, Tommy. What do you know about this murder, eh?'

'Nuthin',' declared Mr. Custer, in alarm. 'I don't know nuthin' about it. So don't you go tryin' to pin anythin' on *me* . . . '

'Don't you go worryin' yerself,' said Mr. Budd, reassuringly. 'If you're going straight you've got nothin' to fear from me. Now you just pop along an' tell Mr. Brockwell that we're 'ere and 'ud like to see him.'

'You'd better come in,' said Tom Custer, uneasily. 'An' look 'ere — Mr. Brockwell don't know anythin' about my past . . . '

'That's all right,' broke in Mr. Budd, cheerfully. 'He won't learn about it from me — so long as you be'ave yourself and don't get up to any tricks.'

The disconcerted and apprehensive Mr. Custer led them into a room opening off the hall — an atrocious place of gilt and plush — and left them.

'Do you seriously mean that that man is a criminal?' asked Major Toppington.

'Yes, sir,' replied the big superintendent. 'He's been through our hands twice. Maybe he's reformed, as 'e says, but I doubt it. Fellers like him couldn't run straight if they tried. It ain't in 'em . . .'

'Do you think he can have anything to do with this business?' asked the Chief Constable, and Mr. Budd shook his head.

'No, sir,' he replied. 'Custer's no killer . . .'

He broke off as the subject of the conversation came back.

'Will you come with me?' he said. 'Mr. Brockwell's in the drawin'-room.'

They followed him across the huge pillared hall to a door that faced the room

29

they had just left.

'Now don't you go giving me away,' hissed Mr. Custer, urgently. 'I'm not doin' nuthin' again' the law workin' for me livin' . . . '

'I won't, Tom,' murmured Mr. Budd, 'unless I find out that you're up to any of your old games, an' then you'd better watch out.'

Tom Custer grunted, tapped on the door, opened it, stood aside, and announced: 'Sup'ntendent Budd and Major Topping-ton.'

The room was enormous and furnished with the ornate ugliness of an hotel lounge. There was a profusion of gilt and damask straight from Tottenham Court Road, and the walls were hung with great mirrors that reached from floor to ceiling and made the room look larger than it really was. In this hideous apartment were four people. Before the fireplace, in which a log fire blazed, stood a short, stout man dressed in plus-fours of a blatant check pattern. His coarse face was the colour of a new brick and his hair was very short and of a fiery red. He stood with his thumbs in the armholes of his waistcoat and his thick legs very wide apart: a dominating, rather brutal-looking figure. Leaning back against the cushions of a large settee was a woman. She was thin and very bony, with hair of a ridiculous shining gold, and she was made up so thickly that it appeared as if she had applied it with a trowel. In a chair, reading a book, with a box of sweets on her lap was a girl — quite a good-looking girl in a flamboyant way, but with a sullen, rather sulky set to her full mouth. The fourth occupant of the room was a lanky youth with a pimply face and red hair plastered smoothly down to his narrow skull. With his hands thrust into his pockets he stood and gaped at them, his loose mouth half-open. The Chief Constable had been right, thought Mr. Budd, as his sleepy eyes took all this in. A very queer lot indeed.

'Come in, Toppington,' greeted the man in front of the fire, in a rough, uncultured voice. 'So this is the chap from Scotland Yard, is it? 'Ow d'you do. I hope you're going to make a better go of

31

it than the locals.'

'I'll do everythin' I can, sir,' said Mr. Budd, quietly.

'I 'ope it gets us somewhere,' was the ungracious retort. 'So far nothing 'as been done and it's over three weeks since my son was killed . . . '

'We have done our best, Mr. Brockwell,' put in the Chief Constable.

'An' a precious poor best it's been,' growled Henry Brockwell, rudely. 'I 'ope this feller can produce somethin' better in the way of results, that's all.' He looked at Mr. Budd with his small, red-rimmed eyes as though he were inspecting cattle.

'There are one or two questions I should like to ask you,' said the big man.

'Ask away,' answered Mr. Brockwell, curtly. 'This is my wife . . . ' He jerked his head towards the woman on the settee. 'That's my daughter and that's my son. Now what d'you want to know?' He did not suggest that they should sit down. He was obviously completely lacking in even the rudiments of hospitality.

'Well, sir,' said Mr. Budd. 'That's easily answered. To begin with I should like you ter tell me anything that might have a bearin' on this unfortunate business . . . '

'An' that's nothing,' said Brockwell. 'D'you think if I knew anything — if any of us knew anything — we shouldn't have told Toppington 'ere, an' Tidworthy?'

Mr. Budd adopted his most bovine and sleepy expression.

'I s'pose you would,' he remarked, rubbing his chin. 'Well, then, p'raps I'd better begin by askin' you if your son had any enemies?'

'Quite a lot of people didn't like 'im,' replied Mr. Brockwell, 'but not so badly that they'd want to murder 'im . . . '

'I'm not so sure of *that*,' put in the pimply youth, with a sneer.

'You 'old yer blasted tongue!' snapped his father, angrily. 'Nobody's talkin' to you . . . '

'I'm goin' to talk to him, though,' said Mr. Budd. 'What's your name, young feller?'

'Look here . . . ' began Henry Brockwell, but the big man stopped him with an authoritative gesture.

'*If* you please, sir,' he said. 'Now then,

what's your name?'

'James Brockwell,' said the pimply youth, sullenly.

'What did you mean by what you said just now?' went on Mr. Budd. 'Do you know of any person who hated your brother enough to want to kill him?'

James Brockwell shifted uneasily from one foot to the other.

'Why don't you tell him, Jimmy?' said the girl, looking up from her book suddenly. 'Why don't you say that you hated John and would probably have killed him yourself, only you haven't got the pluck of a louse . . . '

'Sandra!' Mrs. Brockwell spoke sharply, but without moving. 'You shut yer mouth, d'yer 'ear?' The voice was dreadful, harsh, nasal, and with a hideous twang. Mr. Budd began to think that when the Chief Constable had called them 'queer' he had been guilty of an understatement.

'I'll talk if I want to,' retorted Sandra. 'It's no secret that Jimmy and Johnny hated each other — almost as much as I hate 'em both . . . '

'That'll do, my gal,' interposed Mr.

Brockwell. 'This ain't goin' ter 'elp at all. Don't take any notice of what *they* say,' he continued, turning to Mr. Budd. 'You know 'ow it is among brothers and sisters? . . . It don't mean anythin' really . . . '

Mr. Budd wasn't at all sure about that, but for the time being he was prepared to agree. Sandra shot a venomous look at her father, shrugged her shoulders, and returned to her book and her sweets. James, with a sheepish grin, turned away and stared at the broad, high windows which filled the entire end of the room.

'I take it, then,' murmured Mr. Budd, 'that you don't know of any motive for your youngest son's death?'

'No,' said Mr. Brockwell, shortly.

'Have you any idea,' continued the stout superintendent, 'why he went to this place, Cooper's Spinney, at such an hour?'

'No,' said Mr. Brockwell again. Sandra half-raised her head as though she were going to say something, thought better of it, and went on reading, though Mr. Budd would have been willing to bet a considerable sum that she had no idea what the printed page before her was about.

'How far is Cooper's Spinney from 'ere?' asked Mr. Budd, and it was Major Toppington who answered him.

'About a mile,' he said.

'Was your son out or in durin' the evenin'?' said Mr. Budd, turning again to Brockwell.

'In,' he answered. ''E went out earlier, but 'e was back for dinner. I'd no idea he went out again. 'E said he was goin' to bed.'

'What time did the rest of you go to bed that night?' said Mr. Budd.

'I went to bed h'early,' replied Mrs. Brockwell. 'I'd 'ad an 'eadache all the h'evening. Just about ten it was when I went h'upstairs.'

'Thank you, ma'am,' murmured Mr. Budd, politely, 'an' you, miss?'

'Me?' Sandra raised her eyes languidly. 'I wasn't here at all. I spent the night in London . . .'

'Don't ask her where,' said James, looking round with a leer. 'She might feel

36

embarrassed . . . '

'You be quiet, you little nit!' shouted his sister, flaming into a sudden rage.

'I'll bash your face in, if you talk to me like that!' cried James Brockwell, coming towards her threateningly.

'You try it, that's all.' Sandra sprang up, her book and sweets falling to the floor. 'You touch me an' I'll . . . '

'Stop it!' Henry Brockwell, his face purple with rage, stepped forward, gripped his daughter by the arm and shook her violently.

'Let go of me!' she screamed, lashing out at his shins with her high heels. 'Let go! You're hurting me . . . '

'I'll break your blasted neck if you don't shut up,' threatened her father, furiously. 'Now sit down an' be'ave.' He flung her into the chair, and James gave a high-pitched laugh.

'That's right,' he said. 'Give . . . '

'You shut up, too!' snarled Brockwell, swinging round on him, 'or I'll give *you* something you won't forget in a 'urry!'

James shrank back. He was not, apparently, of the stuff of which heroes are made. Sandra glared at him, rubbing her bruised arm, but she said nothing more.

'Well, now,' said Mr. Budd, stolidly, when this agreeable glimpse of family life among the Brockwells had faded. 'You, ma'am, went to bed at ten o'clock, an' you, miss, were in London . . . '

'I wasn't at home either,' said James, quickly. 'I stayed with a friend at Bedlington.'

'I see. Well, that leaves you, sir,' said Mr. Budd, looking at Brockwell.

'I don't know what time I went to bed,' he answered. 'I had one or two drinks and sat up smoking after the h'others had gone. Round about twelvish, I s'pose. What good are all these questions?'

'I'm just tryin' ter get some idea of what happened,' explained the big man. 'It looks to me as though your son must 'ave had an appointment with somebody at Cooper's Spinney — an appointment that he didn't want any of the household to know about . . . '

'That's quite likely,' interrupted James, with a sneering laugh, 'and I'll bet it was some girl or other. John was a great one for sneakin' out at night to meet girls . . . '

'You couldn't suggest who it might have bin?' asked Mr. Budd, and James shook his narrow head.

'No, I can't,' he answered. 'Some little trollop from the village, I expect. Now, if it had been Sandra, I *might* have been able . . . '

'You shut your great mouth!' cried his sister, furiously.

'Don't start that all over again,' cut in Brockwell. 'You won't get anywhere this way,' he went on to Mr. Budd. 'We don't know h'anything. If John 'ad an appointment with somebody we don't know who it was . . . '

There was a tap at the door and Tom Custer entered nervously.

'What do you want?' snarled Mr. Brockwell, irritably.

'I've just found this in the 'all, sir,' said Custer, and held out an envelope. 'It's addressed to you, sir . . . '

'You should 'ave brought h'it on a salver — a silver salver,' said Mrs.

Brockwell, severely, and James sniggered.

Henry Brockwell snatched the envelope from the servant's hand, glared at it, and tore it open.

'What's all this tomfoolery?' he growled, glancing at the sheet of paper it had contained. ''Ow did this get 'ere?'

'I don't know, sir,' answered Custer. 'I just found it. It wasn't there when these gen'l'men come . . . '

'Do you know anythin' about this?' Brockwell thrust the sheet of paper at Mr. Budd. The big man took it, looked at it, and his thick lips pursed themselves. On the paper were five lines of printed characters that ran:

THE TEN OF DIAMONDS
THE JACK OF DIAMONDS
THE QUEEN OF DIAMONDS
THE KING OF DIAMONDS
THE ACE OF DIAMONDS

Beside the Ten of Diamonds a cross had been heavily drawn in pencil.

'H'm,' remarked Mr. Budd, thoughtfully, pinching his fleshy chin. 'Queer, ain't it? Ten, Jack, Queen, King, Ace . . . If I was playin' poker an' I had a 'and like that I'd bet me last 'a' penny . . . '

'A royal flush,' grunted Henry Brock-well. 'A royal . . . '

He stopped abruptly and the big man saw his face change. The brick-red colour slowly drained away, leaving behind a dirty yellow hue.

'Yes, sir,' he murmured. 'As you say, a royal flush. The most significant thing about it, though, is this cross against the Ten of Diamonds. It was the Ten of Diamonds that was found pinned on the dead body of your son, wasn't it?'

4

Mr. Budd sat in a corner of the bar at the Peal o' Bells and sipped approvingly at the contents of a pint pewter tankard. When he and Major Toppington had left the extravagantly ornate home of the Brockwells it was growing dusk, and the first consideration had been where the big superintendent and the melancholy Sergeant Leek could find accommodation. The Chief Constable had suggested Bedlington, but Mr. Budd decided that he would prefer something nearer to the scene of his activities. He liked, if possible, to be on the spot where he could make the acquaintance of everybody who might be, even remotely, connected with the inquiry on which he was engaged, and gather all the gossip that was going about. On more than one occasion in the past he had found this an advantage and, of course, the ideal place was the local pub. When, therefore, on the way back to Bedlington — he had to take the Chief Constable back and pick up Leek, whom he had left at the police station — he saw the Peal o' Bells, he suggested that they should stop for a drink and see if the place would put him up.

Mr. George Duffy, the landlord, a large and good-humoured man, supplied Major Toppington with a double Johnnie Walker and Mr. Budd with a pint of very good beer, and said that he had one room which he would be very pleased to place at the big man's disposal. He went on to say that if he was looking for further accommodation for his friend, Mrs. Cutts — who lived a few minutes' walk away — had a spare room in her cottage and would be only too glad to 'look after' him.

Mr. Budd went along and saw Mrs. Cutts, while the Chief Constable ordered two more drinks, and the arrangements were completed. He brought Leek back with him, installed him in the cottage, and returned to the Peal o' Bells to eat the substantial meal which Mrs. Duffy had cooked for him. A little tired, but feeling placid and contented, he then repaired to the bar, settled himself with

his beer in a comfortable corner, and —
with one of his strong, evil-smelling
cigars, stuck between his teeth — allowed
himself to ruminate over the events of the
day and to pick up any stray information
that might come his way.

When you stepped across the threshold
of the Peal o' Bells it was like stepping
into another and better age. The place
was very old and gave the impression that
nothing in it had changed during the past
two hundred years. Even Mr. Duffy, who
was not more than fifty-odd, fitted the
place so perfectly that he might have been
the original landlord, and it was possible
to imagine the gritty feeling of sand under
your feet. The contrast with the outside
world was very marked and Mr. Budd
wondered whether that world with its
bustle and confusion, its jostling and
elbowing and raucous noise, *was* such a
great improvement on the old. *Were*
people happier in this new world than
they had been in the old? Did faster
means of transport, better plumbing,
chromium plate, and vita glass — all the
amenities that science had brought to this

modern age — really make for greater happiness? Did all this compensate for that lost contentment, that inward peace that had been but was no more? Were the people of the great towns — regimented, controlled, dry-nursed throughout their lives by this union or that — carefree and merry and full of the joyousness of life? If they were, thought Mr. Budd, they had a queer way of showing it. Always grumbling, downing tools, and striking on the slightest provocation and sometimes without any provocation at all, resentful and continually at loggerheads with their employers and themselves. Never satisfied, always demanding more of this and more of that, and still discontented when they got it. He had seen these people making such gigantic and hysterical efforts to enjoy themselves in a kind of desperate hope that if they made enough noise about it they could deceive even themselves into the belief that they were having a good time. But were they happy? Now that they had got a good deal of what they had so persistently demanded, were they more contented or really better off? He very much doubted it. Happiness — contentment — comes from within. It was a state of mind, and these people's minds were no longer a breeding-place for it. They were like the inmates of a huge asylum for the insane in which the doctors, nurses, and attendants had themselves gone mad . . .

These people of Long Millford, congregated in the cosy bar of the Peal o' Bells, seemed to have achieved that quiet satisfaction with life which the great majority had missed and were so diligently seeking. They weren't worrying their lives away trying to squeeze another tuppence or threepence an hour, or an extra ten bob a week in their wage packets. They weren't envious and discontented because somebody else was getting a little more than they were. They lived happily within the limits of their various positions, joining in with zest and enthusiasm in the community life of the village. A fine lot of men from the old stock that had made Britain great.

Mr. Budd finished his pint of beer and went and fetched himself another. Several curious glances were shot at him, and he concluded that Mr. Duffy had probably told his customers who he was and what he was there for. The murder must have created quite a stir in a tiny place like Long Millford, where there would be little to disturb the placid flow of life.

He had just settled back in his corner when a man came into the bar quickly. He was tall and dark and well dressed. He called for a Johnnie Walker and Mr. Duffy greeted him with an expansive smile.

'Good evenin', doctor,' he said. 'Haven't seen you for a long time.'

'No, I've been kept fairly busy,' said the newcomer, in a pleasant voice. 'Scarcely time to eat, much less drink.'

'It's this 'ere 'flu, I s'pose?' remarked the landlord, setting down the whisky in front of his customer and pushing forward a syphon of soda. 'Queer 'ow it seems to come on just at this time o' the year.'

'It's not so queer, really,' said the dark man, squirting a little soda-water into his glass. 'The weather gets a bit warmer, and people grow careless. How's your wife, Mason?'

'Pretty nigh well again, thank you, Doctor Middlesham,' replied a red-faced, stocky man. 'That stuff you give her was 'orrible bitter, but it did 'er a powerful lot o' good.'

'There's no such thing as nice medicine,' said the newcomer, with a smile. 'The nastier it is the better it is.'

So this was Doctor Middlesham, thought Mr. Budd. He'd been the first to examine the body of John Brockwell. Sensible-looking sort of chap. Not very old, either. Round about thirty or thirty-five by the look of him. The doctor looked in his direction at that moment, caught his eye, and said something to the landlord in a lower tone. Mr. Duffy glanced across at Mr. Budd and replied. Doctor Middlesham picked up his glass and came over to the big man's corner.

'I understand you're from Scotland Yard?' he said. 'Come down to investigate young Brockwell's murder?'

'That's right, sir,' replied Mr. Budd, nodding slowly. 'You're the doctor what first examined the body — Doctor Middlesham?'

'Yes, nasty business.' Middlesham made

48

a wry face at the recollection. 'Strange affair altogether. I hope you get to the bottom of it.'

'I 'ope so too, sir,' said Mr. Budd.

'Not that I've got any sympathy with the victim,' went on Middlesham. 'John Brockwell was a nasty piece of work in every way — like the rest of 'em. It 'ud be a good thing for the world in general, and this place in particular, if somebody murdered the lot. That's my opinion.'

'That 'ud apply to quite a lot o' people,' said Mr. Budd. 'But you can't let 'em be murdered indiscriminately, all the same, sir.'

'No, of course you can't,' said Middlesham. He gulped down his whisky. 'I'm going to have another,' he said. 'What will you have — er — Inspector, is it?'

'Sup'n'tendent, sir,' replied the big man. 'Sup'n'tendent Budd . . . I'll 'ave a pint of beer, thank you.'

Doctor Middlesham went over to the bar, and Mr. Budd's sleepy eyes followed him speculatively. Seemed to be quite a nice feller, he thought. Very ready to be friendly. Obviously he didn't like the

49

Brockwells, but that wasn't very surprising. Mr. Budd imagined that there would be few people who would. Was it *only* a desire to be friendly that had prompted him to come and make himself agreeable directly he had learned who the stranger was? Or was there something more behind it than that? The big man decided that he was quite interested in Doctor Middlesham.

He came back with another Johnnie Walker for himself and a tankard of beer for Mr. Budd.

'Well, here's luck, Superintendent,' he said, holding up his glass.

'I shall need it, sir,' said Mr. Budd, fervently. 'I 'aven't been 'ere very long, of course, but I think I'm in possession of all that's known about this business an' I must say that there ain't much to go on. You was about the first to see the body, wasn't you, sir?'

'Yes.' Middlesham nodded. 'But I'm afraid I can't add to your knowledge much, Superintendent. The prongs of the pitchfork went right through his chest and the force behind the blow must have been pretty powerful . . . '

'I gathered that,' said Mr. Budd. 'Which means that the murderer must have been very strong. That narrows it down a bit. 'Ow tall was Brockwell?'

'Of medium height,' answered Middlesham, looking a little surprised at the question. 'About up to my shoulder.'

'And at what angle 'ad the weapon entered his chest?' asked the big man. 'I mean, was it upward or downward?'

'Slightly downward,' replied the doctor, quickly. 'I see what you're getting at . . . '

'Yes, sir,' said Mr. Budd. 'It gives us some sort of an idea what we've got to look for, don't it? A fairly tall man with unusual strength. Well, that ain't much, but it's somethin'.'

'There are quite a number of people in this district answering to *that* description,' remarked Middlesham.

'I expect so, sir,' agreed Mr. Budd. 'But whoever did this 'as got to have 'ad a motive, an' that's the first thing to look for — unless, of course, there's an 'omicidal lunatic wanderin' about the place . . . '

'That possibility occurred to *me*,' said Middlesham.

'It's got to be taken into account,' said Mr. Budd, thoughtfully. He did not add that he thought such an explanation unlikely. That letter, which had arrived at the Brockwells' so mysteriously, with the queer list of playing-cards making a royal flush, was not like the work of a lunatic. There was only one way in which it could have been delivered without the person who brought it being seen coming or leaving the house, and that was through the auspices of Tommy Custer. Mr. Budd had said nothing at the time, but he had been convinced that Custer was lying when he said he had found the letter in the hall. He had done nothing of the sort. *Somebody* had given it to him and bribed him to deliver it at that specific time . . .

'I don't see . . . ' began Doctor Middlesham, who stopped as the door suddenly opened and a girl came in. She stood for a moment just inside the bar, looking quickly about her, and then she saw Middlesham, smiled, and came over.

'Rita said you'd probably be here, Dick,' she said. 'So I thought I'd come and find you . . . '

'Hello, Clarissa,' said Middlesham, his dark face lighting up with pleasure. 'I say, I'm sorry. I thought I'd get back in plenty of time . . .'

'I'm early, as a matter of fact,' said Clarissa. 'Now I'm here you can buy me a drink — gin and lime, please.'

'Of course.' Doctor Middlesham introduced Mr. Budd hastily, and the big man discovered that the girl was Clarissa Pipp-Parkington, the daughter of Sir Oswald and Lady Pipp-Parkington.

'Are you really a detective?' she said, when Middlesham had gone to get her drink.

'Well, that's what I'm s'posed to be, miss,' replied Mr. Budd, looking at her with a twinkle in his sleepy eyes. 'There 'as bin differences of opinion about it at times . . .'

She laughed, and he thought it made her look very attractive.

'Well, I hope this isn't going to be one of the times,' she said. 'Have you been up to that awful house — the Brockwells' place, I mean?'

He nodded.

'Really ghastly, isn't it? If only you could have seen it before. It was such a lovely old place.' Her face clouded for an instant. 'I was born there. It used to belong to us. But with taxes and things we couldn't afford to keep it, so father had to sell it. If he'd known what Brockwell was going to do to it I'm sure he'd rather have cut off his right hand . . . '

'Here you are, Clarissa.' Middlesham rejoined them with the gin and lime. 'Why didn't Rita come with you?'

'She was in the middle of making cakes,' said Clarissa. 'The smell was delicious . . . '

'She's not a bad cook,' remarked Middlesham.

'Not bad?' echoed Clarissa. 'I should jolly well say she isn't. I wish Mrs. Bowling was a quarter as good. I don't think you appreciate your sister as much as you should, Dick.'

So Rita's his sister, eh, thought Mr. Budd. And this girl seems likely to become something closer before very long. From under his drooping lids he took stock of her. Nice-looking, good figure, though a little on the thin side. Lovely eyes, very dark — almost as dark as her glossy hair . . . Really beautiful when she laughed . . . Mentally he catalogued her attractions . . .

'Well, we ought to be going,' said Middlesham, finishing his drink. 'Come along, Clarissa. Glad I met you, Superintendent. I expect we shall be running into each other again pretty soon. I usually drop in here for a drink during the evening when I'm not too busy.'

'The next time it'll be my turn to buy you one,' said Mr. Budd. 'Good night, sir. Good night, miss.'

He watched them as they went out, followed by a chorus of good nights from the other occupants of the bar, and then, finishing the remainder of his beer, he said good night to Mr. Duffy and made his way slowly and ponderously to his room.

5

Comfortably ensconced in a bed that smelt faintly of lavender, with a lighted candle on the table by his side and a cigar clamped between his teeth, Mr. Budd allowed his massive body to relax and reviewed the events of the day in lazy contentment.

There was no doubt that he was going to find himself up against a tough proposition this time — a very tough proposition. So far he could see no clear line of inquiry to follow. He would just have to nose around and hope that something would happen to give him a lead. After three weeks of energetic effort on the part of Tidworthy there would be very little ground that hadn't been covered. It was true that he had found something that they — the local police — had overlooked, but that was due to previous knowledge. They couldn't have been expected to identify Tommy Custer.

The question was, did Tommy Custer fit into this business? Mr. Budd was inclined to think that he didn't. Or, if he did, only in a very minor capacity. Custer was, quite certainly, not the type of crook to get himself tangled up with a murder. He might pinch the spoons and the silver and any other valuables that happened to be lying around, but he wouldn't get mixed up with anything that approached violence. A peaceable feller in his way, was Tommy, and always had been. But he must have been responsible for the discovery of that queer note, which meant that somebody had given it to him.

Now who could it have been? Certainly not the murderer. If Tommy had had any idea that it *might* have been the murderer, he wouldn't have touched it with a barge pole. Therefore it must have been given him by someone whom he knew was above suspicion. Yet the note was very definitely connected with the murder. A playing-card, the ten of diamonds, had been found pinned to the jacket of the dead man, and the note was a list of the diamond suit, from the ace to the ten.

A nap hand or a royal flush in poker. What did it mean? Something to Henry Brockwell, apparently, that was unpleasant, for his face had gone almost grey. Something that had only occurred to him when Mr. Budd had mentioned the word 'poker.' What meaning could it have? What memory had the sight of a royal flush in diamonds set loose?

A queer, strange family the Brockwells. There was very little sign of grief over the death of the youngest son. Unnatural when you came to think of it — or, maybe, not so unnatural when you knew the people concerned. A bickering, quarrelling lot, common as dirt . . . What had induced them to settle down in a place like Long Millford, and build that monstrosity of a house? It was the last place you would expect to find such people. There was nothing there to appeal to them. They were the kind who should have been more at home in a town among night-clubs, dance-halls, cinemas, and all the hectic excitements that a town could have offered. They were as out of place in this rural retreat, tucked away from the rest of the world, as a hermit in the middle of Piccadilly Circus.

So why had they come here? It might be very enlightening to find out. There was quite a lot he would like to find out about the Brockwells, Mr. Budd decided. That was the best angle to attack this business, because he felt that the solution to the murder was more likely to be discovered that way. It was no hot-headed crime of passion carried out on the spur of the moment, but a cold-blooded, calculated killing, carefully planned in advance. Young John Brockwell had been decoyed to Cooper's Spinney on some pretext or other, and there the murderer had been waiting for him, armed with the stolen pitchfork . . . And there had been no signs of a struggle. Brockwell had not expected death to spring at him out of the dark and silence of that little wood. Death had come in a friendly guise . . .

Mr. Budd yawned, crushed out the remains of his cigar in the cracked saucer which did duty for an ashtray, and blew out the candle . . .

6

Sergeant Leek found his quarters with Mrs. Cutts very comfortable indeed. That rotund and beaming lady had welcomed him on his arrival as though he had been the prodigal son; and if she had not, in actual fact, killed the fatted calf, she had provided him with a supper that left nothing to be desired.

His bed was soft and downy, into which his lean form sank between mountains of feathers, and there was a hot-water bottle to take the initial chill from the sheets. Compared with his own rather shabby and dreary bed-sitting-room in the Kennington Road it was luxury, and he decided that the longer the investigation took into the murder of John Brockwell the better he would be pleased. When he came to this decision he had not met Ginger. That was a pleasure to be mercifully deferred until the morning.

He came down to breakfast at eight

o'clock in a mood of quiet content, which was the nearest he ever got to cheerfulness, and which only happened on an average once in every five years. He was greeted by a hideous and bloodcurdling yell, as he reached the foot of the narrow staircase, which startled him so much that he slipped, stumbled down the three remaining stairs, and very nearly fell into the little parlour.

'Stick 'em up!' screamed a voice in shrill command, and a small figure with flaming red hair and a freckled face appeared from the concealment of the coat-rack, brandishing a very ancient pistol. 'Got you!'

'Look here . . . ' began Leek, breathlessly.

'Can it!' snapped the small apparition, curtly, and he jabbed the hard barrel of the pistol into the unfortunate Leek's stomach with no gentle hand. The sergeant gave a gasp of pain and almost doubled up.

'Did yer think you'd git the better o' Black 'awk?' cried the small boy, triumphantly, grinding the pistol harder and

61

harder into Leek's solar plexus. 'Stick up yer 'ands . . . '

'Take that thing away,' grunted the sergeant. 'What d'you think you're doin'?'

'I've bin waiting fer yer,' hissed the small boy, screwing up his face into an expression of fiendish rage. 'Black 'awk knows all!'

'Oh, does 'e?' said Leek, grasping the pistol and forcibly removing it from his tender anatomy. 'Well, Black Hawk 'ad better know a bit more, an' learn that 'e can't go about yellin' and stickin' things into people . . . '

'Leggo!' cried the boy. 'Leggo, or I'll fill yer full of lead!'

'Ginger! Whatever are you doing, you bad boy?' Mrs. Cutts appeared in the doorway of the parlour with a laden tray. 'What's 'e bin doing, sir?'

'Nuthin' very much,' said Leek, escaping thankfully and sitting down at the breakfast table. 'Just a little game, that's all . . . '

'I'll give him gimes,' broke in Mrs. Cutts. 'You go along an' wash yerself, Ginger, an' get ready fer school, an' remember you're not to annoy people . . . '

'I wasn't doin' nuthin',' muttered Ginger, looking at his mother sullenly.

'I 'eard you screamin' the place down,' said Mrs. Cutts. 'Black 'awk, indeed! It's all these 'comics' an' penny 'bloods' you're always a-readin'. Fillin' yer head with a lot o' trash. Now just you run along an' don't forget to wash yer neck an' yer ears.'

The dreaded 'Black Hawk' slunk reluctantly away.

'If 'e starts annoyin' yer, sir,' said Mrs. Cutts, 'you just land 'im one. It'll be doin' me a favour. 'E's more'n what I can cope with sometimes.' She had been transferring the contents of the tray to the table while she was speaking, and now she stood back to admire her handiwork. 'If there's anything else you should want, sir, will you give a call?'

Leek assured her that he would and she left him to tackle the substantial breakfast which she had prepared for him. He was halfway through the meal when the door was cautiously pushed open and Ginger thrust his head in. His hair was still an unruly mop, but his face was clean and shining rosily.

'I say,' he said, in a hoarse whisper. 'Is it true?'

'What?' asked Leek, eyeing him warily.

Ginger edged himself further into the room, squirming delicately round the half-open door.

'Mum says yer a 'tec,' he whispered, excitedly. 'From Scotland Yard . . . '

'That's right,' said the sergeant.

'Coo!' Ginger wriggled ecstatically. ''Ave you got a gun — a real gun — one o' them automatics?'

Leek shook his thin head.

'No, sonny,' he replied. 'We ain't allowed ter carry firearms — only by special permission.'

'Oh!' Ginger was obviously disappointed. 'Yer can't be much of a 'tec if yer 'aven't got a gun,' he declared, candidly. 'Sexton Blake always carried a gun, an' so did Tinker. You know *them*, of course . . . ?'

'Can't say I do,' said Leek.

'You don't know Sexton Blake an' Tinker?' cried Ginger, incredulously. 'Coo, I thought everybody knew 'em at the Yard.' His large eyes narrowed and he regarded Leek suspiciously. ''Ere, I s'pose yer *is* from the

Yard?' he said. 'You ain't bin tellin' mum lies, 'ave yer?'

The melancholy sergeant assured him that he had not been deceiving the worthy Mrs. Cutts, but his assurance did not seem to make a great deal of impression on Ginger.

'Don't seem right ter me,' he muttered, wrinkling his small forehead. 'You ain't got no gun an' you don' know . . . '

'Ginger, why aren't you on your way to school?' Mrs. Cutts peered in through the partly open door. 'You run along at once an' leave the gentleman to have 'is breakfast in peace and quietness. Now go along with you or you'll be late . . . '

'I got plen'y o' time,' said Ginger.

'You do as you're told, an' don't argue,' said his mother. 'Now git along . . . '

Ginger reluctantly departed, and Leek heard his mother scolding him for worrying 'the gentleman.' With a sigh he continued his interrupted breakfast, concluding that it might not turn out to be so pleasant and peaceful at Mrs. Cutts's cottage as he had at first believed.

He was in the tiny garden staring

gloomily at some daffodils that were partially in bloom, when Mr. Budd arrived.

'Hello,' greeted the big man. ' 'Ave you taken up botany, or are yer just feelin' poetic?'

'I was thinkin' . . . ' began Leek.

'Were you now?' said Mr. Budd, in astonishment. 'Well, that's a change, anyhow. I'm sorry to interrupt you, but we are down 'ere for a job o' work . . . '

'What d'you want me ter do?' asked Leek.

'I'm goin' along to 'ave a look at Cooper's Spinney where this Brockwell feller was stuck with the pitchfork,' said Mr. Budd, producing a cigar and sniffing at it in pleasurable anticipation. 'An' I want you to come along with me.'

'All right,' said Leek. 'I'll just run up an' get me 'at . . . ' He ambled slowly towards the house with his usual shambling gait.

'For a moment I thought you meant it,' called the big man. 'If that's what yer call runnin' what do yer do when you walk?'

The lean sergeant made no answer, but he quickened his pace slightly and disappeared inside the cottage. When, after the lapse of a couple of minutes, he rejoined Mr. Budd, he found him chatting pleasantly to Mrs. Cutts. The big man seemed in no particular hurry to start for Cooper's Spinney. Mrs. Cutts, like the majority of her kind, only required an appreciative audience to release the pent-up stream of her volubility, and Mr. Budd was being very appreciative just then. While Leek fidgeted in the background, he listened to a great deal of very interesting information concerning the village and its inhabitants, putting in a murmured word now and again every time the stream threatened to dry up. It was nearly half an hour later before he and Leek set off for their original destination.

'Why did you waste your time listenin' to all that?' said Leek, as they walked up the road.

'It wasn't a waste of time,' answered Mr. Budd, lighting the cigar which he had been rolling thoughtfully between his fingers while he listened to Mrs. Cutts. 'I've learned more about the district an' the people from that woman than I'd 've done from a couple o' hours' questioning.

If you can find a natural gossip an' just let 'em ramble on, you always learn more than what you would if you 'ave to ask a lot o' questions. There's sump'n about questions which dries people up . . . '

'Well, I don't see that you've learned much that's any good,' said the sergeant.

''Ow do you know what's goin' ter be good an' what's not?' demanded Mr. Budd. 'If you do, you're cleverer than what I am. We're investigatin' a murder an' the more we know about the background the better. An' the background means the people who live in this district an' all about 'em. I'll agree that a lot of the information'll be useless, but we don't know which, an' we shan't know which, until we've found out why young Brockwell was killed an' who killed him.'

Leek admitted, a little grudgingly, that perhaps he was right. ''Ow far is this place, Cooper's Spinney?' he asked.

''Bout a quarter of a mile the other side of the village,' replied his superior. 'You can only get to it through a narrow lane an' along the side of a ploughed field, or I should 'ave brought me car. What's the matter? You can't be feelin' tired already . . . '

'I only wanted ter know where it was,' said Leek, but his face lengthened at the prospect of walking so far. 'What d'you think of this business?'

Mr. Budd took the cigar from between his teeth and pushed his soft-brimmed hat further back on his head. It was a warm morning and the unaccustomed exercise was making him hot.

'It looks as if it might be difficult,' he remarked, slowly. 'Very difficult. I'm not even beginnin' to think about it yet. I'm just goin' to collect all the information I can an' hope that I'll pick up somethin' that'll give me a line. D'you remember Tommy Custer?'

Leek wrinkled his forehead.

'Tommy Custer?' he repeated, and shook his thin head. 'No, can't say that I do. Who is 'e?'

Mr. Budd explained, and the lean sergeant's face cleared.

'Oh, yes, now I know who you mean,' he said.

'Well, he's 'ere,' said Mr. Budd. ''E's

got a job as butler with the Brockwells . . . '
He related how he had discovered the disconcerted Mr. Custer.

'I'll bet he's the feller we want,' declared Leek, with conviction. 'I wouldn't bother to look no further . . . '

'I don't s'pose you would,' snapped Mr. Budd. 'An' you'd be wrong. Tommy ain't the feller. Tommy Custer couldn't kill a fly . . . '

'Then what's 'e doin' 'ere?' demanded the sergeant.

'I don't know,' answered Mr. Budd. 'Maybe 'e'll tell us later on, or maybe we'll find out for ourselves.'

He lapsed into silence, puffing jerkily at his cigar, and Leek, recognizing from the signs that his superior was pursuing a train of thought, refrained from interruption. In silence they came at last to Cooper's Spinney. It was a fairish size, but Mr. Budd had no difficulty in finding the tree to which John Brockwell had been pinned like a butterfly to a sheet of cork. The big elm tree stood by itself in a tiny clearing, and the trunk still bore the marks where the prongs of the pitchfork had entered the bark.

'I don't suppose we'll find anything after all this time,' murmured the big man. 'An' Tidworthy an' the locals will 'ave made a pretty thorough search, I expect, but still you never can tell. Takin' this tree as the centre, we'll work round in widenin' circles an' see what we can find.'

'What are we lookin' for?' asked Leek.

'Anything,' answered Mr. Budd. 'Anythin' that might be a clue . . . ' He began to move slowly away, circling the elm, his sleepy eyes on the ground. It was very damp here and the ground was covered with a thick layer of rotten leaves from the previous autumn. He was not very optimistic. If there had been anything to find, it was more than likely that the local police would have found it three weeks earlier. But the big superintendent was thorough and he had no intention of neglecting even the most remote chance. If anything *had* been overlooked, he might be lucky enough to stumble on it.

So engrossed did he become in his task that he was quite unaware that he was being overlooked until a voice, low and clear and musical, and with a hint of laughter in it, said:

'Scotland Yard at work! How very, very interesting!'

7

Mr. Budd looked up and round towards the direction from which the voice had come. He saw, standing a few yards away and watching him with her head slightly on one side, a slim girl of medium height dressed in a pair of fawn-coloured slacks and a lemon-yellow pullover. Leek had gone farther afield and become lost to view in a thicket.

'Good mornin', miss,' said Mr. Budd.

'Good morning,' answered the girl. 'To save you the trouble of asking the question, I'm Harriet Lake.'

'Thank you, miss,' said Mr. Budd, a little taken aback. 'I'm Sup'n'tendent Budd of . . . '

'I know,' interrupted the girl, calmly. 'You're trying to find out who killed that appalling little worm, John Brockwell. I hope you don't! Personally I think the person who killed him should be rewarded very handsomely. But I don't suppose we agree on that point . . . '

'Well, miss, murder's murder, even if the victim's unpopular,' remarked Mr. Budd, 'an' . . . '

'Vermin should be exterminated,' said Harriet Lake. 'If all the Brockwells were put in a lethal chamber it would be a blessing to civilization!'

'You don't appear to like 'em, miss,' said Mr. Budd.

'I hate 'em!' said Harriet Lake, viciously. 'I hate their souls and their guts!'

'May I ask why, miss?' murmured the big man, coming nearer to her.

'You may,' she replied. 'But I don't think I shall tell you. This is a free country and one is entitled to hate whom one pleases.'

'In the circumstances . . . ' began Mr. Budd, and she broke in quickly:

'The circumstances don't make any difference,' she said. '*I* didn't kill the little beast, though I'll admit I've often wanted to — *and* his brother and sister, too!'

Mr. Budd rubbed his chin gently. This vehement and candid young woman interested him. She was quite young — somewhere in the early twenties — and remarkably pretty.

'Do you live in the village, miss?' he inquired.

She nodded.

'Yes, of course,' she said. 'I've a cottage in Mill Lane. I paint pictures for a hobby and do book-jackets, magazine-covers, and black-and-white illustrations for a living. I'm twenty-four years of age, single, and a natural blonde. Now you know all about me.' She looked at him quizzically.

Not by a long chalk, thought Mr. Budd. I know just as much as you want me to know and that's all.

'I see,' he said, aloud. 'Well, miss, I'm very much obliged for the information . . .'

'Don't mention it,' said Harriet. 'I always prefer to volunteer information rather than have it dragged out of me. How are you getting on with the job? Or is that something I shouldn't ask?'

'There's no law to prevent people *askin'* anythin', miss,' said Mr. Budd, politely.

'Tit for tat, eh?' she said, and smiled most attractively. 'Well, if you ever feel that you'd like a quiet cup of tea any afternoon round about four o'clock, just drop in. The first cottage you come to in Mill Lane.'

'Thank you very much, miss,' murmured the big man. 'Maybe I will . . . '

'I hope you will,' she said, seriously. 'Although my sympathies are entirely with the murderer, one doesn't have a murder on the doorstep every day of the week and I'm very interested. I'm rather partial to crime. I think I might have a go at a detective story one of these days. There might be money in it.'

She nodded in a careless, friendly way and sauntered off. Mr. Budd watched her until she was lost to sight among the trees, his brows drawn together and his stubby fingers softly caressing his fat chin.

A strange sort of girl, Miss Harriet Lake, he thought. What was the reason for her hatred of the Brockwells? Maybe she would be worth cultivating, though he very much doubted if he would learn anything she didn't want him to learn. She was a very cool, self-possessed young woman — and yet, perhaps, not quite so cool and self-possessed as she would have people believe. A little overdone, the candour and the casualness? Behind it lurked something else. Fear? No, that was too strong a description. Apprehension? Maybe that was a better word, but still not quite the right one. He continued his search with his mind still on Harriet Lake and he had given it up as fruitless, and was refreshing himself with a cigar, when he found the word he sought. Uneasiness — that was it — uneasiness. But why should she be uneasy? What was the cause? Why should she be worried because a Scotland Yard detective was in the district investigating a murder with which she had no connection? Or *had* she a connection? Was she in some way mixed up with the affair of John Brockwell's killing?

Mr. Budd came to the conclusion that he would be taking advantage of that offer for a quiet cup of tea in Harriet Lake's cottage in the very near future.

8

Sandra Brockwell disappeared during that night. She went out after dinner without telling anyone why or where she was going and she didn't come back. A maid, who always took her up a tray of tea at half-past eight, found her room empty and the bed undisturbed. Mr. Brockwell telephoned the local police at Bedlington and Superintendent Tidworthy and Sergeant Mackleberry came over post-haste, calling at the Peal o' Bells to acquaint Mr. Budd with this latest development. He, in turn, routed out Sergeant Leek, and the four of them drove to The Croft.

They were admitted by Tom Custer. The little man was in a twitter of apprehensive excitement.

'I'm givin' me notice an' clearin' out,' he said. 'I'm not goin' ter get mixed up in this. Cor blimey! Murders an' disappearances! H'I'm off!'

'Oh, no, you're not, Tommy,' said Mr.

Budd, very emphatically. 'You're stayin' put, that's what *you're* doing.'

'Is that a threat?' demanded Mr. Custer, truculently.

'You can take it as you like,' retorted the big man, curtly. 'I should call it a warnin' . . . '

'Ain't this a free country?' said Mr. Custer, with an aggrieved sniff. 'Can't a bloke go where 'e likes?'

'Not a bloke like you,' said Mr. Budd, shaking his head. 'Not a bloke like you, Tommy. If you try an' leave 'ere you'll find yerself in a nice cosy cell in Bedlington p'lice station . . . '

'It's disgraceful!' declared Tommy Custer. 'I ain't done nuthin'. All I want ter do is keep clear o' trouble . . . '

'Well, I'm tellin' yer how to do it,' snapped Mr. Budd. 'Now take us in to Brockwell.'

Mr. Custer, muttering how disgraceful it was under his breath, escorted them to the same room as before. Henry Brockwell was standing in almost the same position in front of the fire, only now he wore a gaudy silk dressing-gown over equally gaudy pyjamas and on his chin was a stubble of beard. Mrs. Brockwell, in a very flimsy and elaborate negligee, was reclining on the settee and James hovered uneasily by the window gnawing at his nails.

'So you've got here at last?' greeted the master of the house hoarsely. 'Took yer time, I must say . . . ' Mr. Budd noticed that his eyes were red and bloodshot and that the hand that plucked nervously at the unshaven chin was shaking. Mr. Brockwell had evidently been fortifying himself from the bottle of Johnnie Walker which stood on a side-table.

'We got here as soon as we could, sir,' said Tidworthy. 'Have you had any news of Miss Brockwell?'

Brockwell shook his head.

'No,' he growled, thickly.

James Brockwell gave a snigger.

'Dunno what you're making all the fuss about,' he sneered. 'She's gone off with one of her boyfriends, that's all . . . '

'You shut up!' cried Mrs. Brockwell, shrilly. 'Hold your tongue!'

'What reason 'ave you got for suggesting that, sir?' asked Mr. Budd.

'He 'asn't got any reason at all,' said his father, roughly.

'Oh, haven't I?' broke in James. 'Well, we shall see who's right, that's all . . . '

'What do *you* think has happened to Miss Brockwell, sir?' Mr. Budd turned his back on the unpleasant youth and addressed Henry Brockwell.

'I don't know. She's gone, that's all I know,' he answered. 'It ain't like her to go off like that without leavin' a message.'

'She always left word when she was goin' away for a day or so,' put in Mrs. Brockwell.

'If she stayed away for good *I* wouldn't lose any sleep,' said James.

'Be quiet!' snapped Brockwell, angrily. 'I don't know what's happened to her an' I'm worried . . . '

You're more than worried, thought Mr. Budd. If ever I've seen a man who was scared to death you're that man.

'There is a chance though, sir, that she may have suddenly remembered an engagement,' said Superintendent Tidworthy. 'When did she leave the house?'

'Soon as we'd 'ad dinner,' replied

Brockwell. 'We none of us saw 'er go. It was Custer who told us she'd gone this mornin'. We thought she'd gone up to her room.'

'Send for Custer,' said Mr. Budd, briefly.

Henry Brockwell went over and rang the bell, pausing on the way back to pour himself out a stiff whisky which he swallowed in a single gulp.

'Why don't you leave that stuff alone?' snapped his wife, and he glared at her but made no reply. There was a knock at the door and Tommy Custer sidled in, his small eyes darting from one to the other suspiciously.

'You saw Miss Brockwell leave last night, is that right?' asked Mr. Budd, without preliminary.

'Yes, that's right,' agreed Mr. Custer. 'I was h'in the 'all when she went h'out.'

'Did she speak to you?'

'No.'

'How was she dressed?'

'Same as what she was at dinner. Sort of a green dress. She'd put a coat h'on over it.'

'What sort of a coat?'

'A thick, lightish-brown thing . . . '

''Er camel-'air coat,' put in Mrs. Brockwell.

'And she just went out without sayin' anythin'?' continued Mr. Budd.

'Tha's right,' agreed Mr. Custer, shifting uneasily from one foot to the other.

James sniffed audibly, but refrained from further comment as he caught his father's eye.

'What time would this be when Miss Brockwell went out?' asked Mr. Budd.

'It was five minutes past eleven,' said Tom Custer. 'I looked at the clock in the 'all.'

'Didn't it strike you as strange that Miss Brockwell should be goin' out at that time?' murmured the big man. 'I mean, so late?'

'No, why should it?' said Mr. Custer. 'She often went out for a bit late like ter get a breather.'

'I see.' Mr. Budd rubbed his chin and then with the knuckle of a fat forefinger tapped gently on the tip of his nose.

'That'll be all, Custer, for the moment.'

Mr. Custer departed with alacrity, obviously only too glad to get away.

'Is there anywhere where your daughter could 'ave gone, sir?' said Mr. Budd. 'Any friends, perhaps, in the village . . . '

'We 'ave no friends in the village,' said Henry Brockwell. 'She knows one or two people over at Bedlington, but she wouldn't 'ave gone there at that time o' night. All the cars is in the garidge . . . '

'P'raps one of her friends came over and fetched her?' suggested Tidworthy. 'With a car, I mean . . . '

'I'll bet you're near it,' said James, with an unpleasant leer. 'That's what I've been sayin' all the time. She'd probably made a date with a boyfriend to meet 'er down the road an' just sneaked out. She'll turn up as large as life with some cock-an'-bull yarn. Trust little Sandra.'

Mr. Budd thought that he was probably right.

'Sandra's never gone away before without sayin' she was going,' said Mrs. Brockwell. 'Not if she was going to stay fer longer'n an hour or so . . . '

'What, in your opinion, has 'appened to her, ma'am?' said Mr. Budd, bluntly, but the woman shook her head.

'I don't know,' she muttered. 'That's your job, ain't it? That's what the p'lice is for, ain't they?'

Superintendent Tidworthy looked at Mr. Budd, but that portly man's eyes were almost completely closed.

'I think it would be advisable, ma'am, to wait before we take any action in the matter,' said Tidworthy, in his best official manner. 'Your daughter may have a very ordinary reason for her absence, and if we start the usual police inquiries it might embarrass her. It's likely that you may be hearing from her before the day's out . . . '

'All right, leave it like that then.' Mr. Brockwell wandered over and picked up the nearly empty bottle of Johnnie Walker. 'Leave it like that. It's your responsibility, though. I've told yer she's gone . . . '

'Put that bottle down, 'Enry,' said his wife, shrilly. 'Put it down, you drunken beast . . . '

'You shut your mouth an' mind your

own business,' snarled Brockwell. 'I'll do as I like, see.'

He tipped the bottle over his glass and emptied it. As he raised the half-full tumbler to his lips, Mrs. Brockwell suddenly sprang up from the settee and knocked it out of his hand. The neat spirit splashed up into his face and eyes and drenched the front of his dressing-gown. With a yell of pain and rage he raised his fist and struck blindly at the woman. The blow caught her on the shoulder and sent her staggering backwards. If Tidworthy hadn't caught her she would have fallen.

'I'll break every bone in your skinny body, you ugly old hag!' snarled Brockwell, rubbing frantically at his eyes with his knuckles. 'I'll smash your face to pulp . . .'

'You'd better go along to the bathroom an' bathe yer eyes,' said Mr. Budd, gripping him by the arm and leading him to the door. 'You won't be able to see until you get the spirit out of 'em . . .' He found Custer in the hall, hovering about suspiciously near the door. 'Here,' he said, 'take your master to the bathroom.

'E's had an accident. Some whisky's got in his eyes . . . '

Tom Custer made a grimace and winked.

'Ain't that dreadful?' he said. 'You 'old on ter me, sir, an' I'll 'ave yer all right in a jiffy.'

Groaning and cursing, Brockwell was helped up the stairs.

9

'What did yer think of that?' said Mr. Budd, as he drove away from The Croft. 'Pretty shockin' exhibition, wasn't it?'

'You're right,' agreed Tidworthy. 'They don't seem to like each other much, do they? This girl, now, I'll bet she's just gone off somewhere on the spree like her brother says. She'll telephone or come back before the day's out. You see.'

But he was wrong. Sandra Brockwell neither telephoned nor put in an appearance, and dusk was merging into darkness when they discovered why.

Part Two

The Knave of Diamonds

1

Ginger hurried home from school as fast as his small legs would carry him. His freckled face, with a smudge of mud across the bridge of his pudgy little nose, was very serious and intent. There was much to be done during the short time that remained before bedtime. He had to have his tea and then get out again in order to preside over a meeting of the 'Hawks,' the gang of which he was the acknowledged leader.

The meeting had been arranged to take place at five-thirty at Weeper's Mill to initiate a new member, one Tommy Potts, the ten-year-old son of the local butcher, and was a most important occasion. Every 'Hawk' had been warned that they must be present on pain of the most dreadful penalties, and bring something towards the banquet which was to follow the fearsome ceremony of initiation. Weeper's Mill, in the days when it had supplied Long Millford with its name, had been a flourishing concern, but for many years now had been derelict and slowly rotting away. The water-wheel had decayed to a few bits of slimy green timber and the shaft and gears which had turned the great stone were a mass of rust. Even the stream which had once flowed with so much life and sparkle was now scarcely more than a brackish trickle, green with weed, its high banks smothered in lush vegetation. There was a cold, dank atmosphere about the place even on the sunniest day, for the great willows that clustered around the ruined building, their drooping branches trailing dejectedly in the stagnant water, kept out all but the barest glimpse of light, and the whole place was, in consequence, plunged in an eternal greenish gloom.

It was ideal as a meeting-place and headquarters for 'The Hawks.' The grinding-chamber with its great stones and rotting sacks of mildewed grain formed, in Ginger's fertile imagination, a weird and gruesome setting for the gang, and equal to anything he had read about in the lurid fiction which he absorbed with so much gusto.

He reached his home, hot, dusty, and with hands and face bearing considerable traces of the geological content of the district. His tea was ready and, after his mother had whisked him off to the sink and scrubbed him clean — a proceeding which he resented with a great deal of vocal protest — he sat down and began to fill himself as rapidly as possible with bread and butter and jam, cake, and weak tea. When Mrs. Cutts was not looking he surreptitiously slipped a couple of cakes into his pocket, and marked down an apple for the same destination, for consumption when the serious business of the day had been completed.

'Where are you goin'?' demanded his mother, as he hastily gulped down a huge mouthful of cake and slid out of his chair.

'Goin' to 'ave a gime with Bob and Willie,' answered Ginger, in a voice that was a trifle choked by the cake which had stuck in his throat.

'Well, you're to be back by seven,' said Mrs. Cutts, severely. 'Now mind, I mean that. Don't you go stayin' out any longer . . . '

'All right,' agreed Ginger, who would have promised anything in order to get away quickly. He wanted to get to Weeper's Mill before the others and light the half-dozen candle-ends which, with much difficulty, he had succeeded in smuggling out of the house on a previous occasion.

'If you're later'n seven,' warned his mother, 'I'll wallop yer . . . '

Ginger bounded upstairs to his bedroom undismayed by the threat. Mrs. Cutts was always threatening him with dire penalties if he didn't do this or that, but they never materialized, and Ginger had learned to treat such signs of attempted authority with contempt. From a drawer he produced the ancient pistol with which he had announced his existence to the astonished Leek, and, rummaging further among the incredible litter, brought to light a long-bladed dagger, his most cherished possession, which had served as a paper-knife until he had coaxed his mother into letting him have it, and was so notched and blunted that it had been useless even for that. Thrusting these into his belt, he picked up a square of black silk with two eyeholes cut in it and clumsily sewn on to a band of elastic, crammed it into a bulging pocket, and completely equipped to become the sinister and dreaded 'Black Hawk,' clattered down the stairs and out of the cottage.

The clock in St. Peter's Church struck five as he set off at a run for Weeper's Mill. It would take him a quarter of an hour, or perhaps a little more, to get there and the meeting had been called for half-past, so he would have plenty of time to get everything ready before the arrival of the gang. It was essential that Tommy Potts should be suitably impressed by his surroundings, and reduced to a condition of respectful awe, before he was officially made a 'Hawk.' Full of plans and schemes, Ginger scuttled along, boldly ignoring the laws of trespass and taking the nearest way across fields and through lanes that had no pretentions to a public right of way. Eventually he arrived within sight of his destination and, dragging the black silk mask from his pocket, put it on over his hot and sticky little face. To reach the old mill it was necessary to cross a shaky wooden bridge. The necessity, it was true, only existed in the vivid imagination of Ginger, since it would have been a great deal easier to cross the stream where its sluggish waters disappeared under a culvert a few yards away, but this was all part of the game. It was also part of the game that he should adopt an air of great caution, as though invisible enemies lurked on every side; and cross the wooden bridge, pistol in hand, alert for the first signs of danger.

At that moment, as he came into the greenish twilight of the clustering willows, he identified himself with all the fictional heroes he had ever read about and became an imaginative composite of them all. The dark opening of the mill loomed up blackly in front of him and he approached it in a half-crouching position, an exaggerated picture of stealth . . .

His small figure disappeared into the yawning darkness of the entrance and was swallowed up. A light flickered and the darkness was faintly and intermittently dispelled . . . And then the small figure came flying out, the mask awry, and the face white and frightened. With great, terrified, sobbing breaths Ginger ran back across the shaking bridge, away from the gloomy mill and the terror which the light of his match had revealed . . .

2

Mr. Budd sat in the corner of the bar at the Peal o' Bells with his usual pint of beer in front of him and wondered whether there would be any news from The Croft. Superintendent Tidworthy had promised to let him know at once if there should be. He had the bar to himself, for it was only a minute past six and Mr. Duffy had only just opened. If the Brockwell family had not been such extraordinary people he might have felt more uneasy over the disappearance of Sandra than he did. But they were such a queer, bad-tempered crew, so completely and utterly selfish, so entirely lacking in any kind of feeling or consideration for each other, that he thought, as James had hinted, that it was quite possible that Sandra was enjoying herself somewhere, and simply not bothering to notify her home.

From the little he had seen of her, Mr.

Budd was quite certain that she wouldn't put herself out to let them know where she was. In similar circumstances they none of them would. There was not the smallest trace of affection in their relationship one to the other. On the contrary, they seemed to regard each other with a sort of contemptuous dislike. It might have been hatred if it hadn't been so cold and unemotional. Definitely a queer family, in which anything might happen and in which murder *had* happened . . .

The door to the bar opened suddenly and the thin form of Leek came in at a shambling run.

''Ullo,' greeted Mr. Budd. 'What's up with you? Don't tell me you've suddenly taken ter drink . . . '

'It's me landlady's kid,' said Leek, breathlessly. 'A boy called Ginger. He's just come runnin' back from a place called Weeper's Mill an' 'e says he found Miss Brockwell there with 'er face all purple . . . '

'What's that?' snapped Mr. Budd, his habitual laziness slipping from him. '*What's that?*'

''E says she's lyin' on a heap of old sacks with 'er face all purple an' swollen,' answered Leek. 'I think the kid's speakin' the truth 'cos he's pretty nearly scared out of his wits . . . '

'When did he tell you this?' demanded the big man.

''Bout a couple o' minutes ago,' answered the sergeant. 'I came round 'ere at once . . . '

'Where's this place, Weeper's Mill?' said Mr. Budd, and Leek shook his head.

'Don't know,' he confessed. 'But it can't be far away . . . '

Mr. Budd got up, drained his tankard, and lumbered over to the door.

'Come on,' he said, curtly, over his shoulder. 'Take me ter this boy . . . '

When they reached the cottage they found the terrified Ginger being soothed by his alarmed mother. Quite evidently he had had a bad shock, for his freckled face was a dirty white and he was shaking with great, shuddering sobs.

'There, there now,' said Mrs. Cutts, pressing him against her ample bosom. 'Nothin's goin' to 'urt you, dear. You shouldn't go playin' around these 'orrid places . . . '

'She was lyin' there on a 'eap of sacks,' sobbed Ginger, jerkily. 'I seed 'er when I struck a match . . . '

'You'd no right to 'ave 'ad matches,' interposed Mrs. Cutts. ''Ow often 'ave I told you not to play with matches . . . ?'

''Er fice was all swollen an' black,' went on Ginger, completely ignoring her rebuke. 'An' 'er eyes was starin' . . . wide open an' starin' . . . '

'Now don't you go thinkin' about it, sonny,' said Mr. Budd, gently. 'Just you tell me where this place, Weeper's Mill, is an' then go off ter bed an' forget all about it.'

'I'll dream about it,' wailed Ginger. 'All poppin' and starin' 'er eyes was . . . ' He broke into an hysterical fit of sobbing, and his mother rocked him back and forth, murmuring that he was quite safe and nothing could harm him, which had no effect whatever.

'I should give 'im a sedative an' put him to bed, ma'am,' advised Mr. Budd. ''Ow do we get to this Weeper's Mill?'

In between repeated admonitions to Ginger to 'stop crying — mother would see that nothin' 'urt him,' Mrs. Cutts issued rather vague directions. Mr. Budd thanked her and took his departure, accompanied by the melancholy Leek. A further inquiry from a farm labourer in the High Street supplied more exact information and they set off for Weeper's Mill.

Mr. Budd was silent and grave. If Ginger was speaking the truth; if he had not imagined the horrible thing he had seen at the old mill, then it looked as if this was another murder. ''Er fice all swollen and black . . . ' That sounded like strangulation . . . First John Brockwell and now Sandra . . . Was someone intent on wiping out the entire Brockwell family? And if so, for what possible reason? Five people and five cards . . . a poker hand . . . a royal flush . . . an unbeatable combination . . . was there some meaning in that? Henry Brockwell had looked as if he thought so. Which meant that he knew something he hadn't divulged . . . Why hadn't he? Didn't he *want* the murderer discovered? No, it couldn't be that. It was he who had practically forced the Chief Constable to call in the assistance of the Yard . . .

A queer business that looked like becoming queerer . . . The big man felt uneasy and not very happy about it all. It was early days yet to offer any sort of an opinion, but at the back of his mind he had an uncomfortable feeling that he might fall down over this case. There was nothing to go on. It was all groping in the dark . . . His gloomy thoughts kept him occupied until they came in sight of Weeper's Mill, and Leek, who had been restraining himself by an almost superhuman effort from breaking in on his superior's obvious desire for silence, burst out suddenly:

'D'you think this gal's been murdered, too?'

''Ow can I tell until we've seen the body?' snarled Mr. Budd, irritably. ''Ow do I know? I don' know that there *is* any gal, yet. The kid may have just seen a heap o' sacks an' imagined the rest.'

'I don't think so,' said Leek, knowing perfectly well that Mr. Budd didn't think so either. 'I'm sure he saw somethin' . . . '

'Somethin' ain't necessarily a dead woman,' grunted Mr. Budd. 'S'pose we wait until we find out definitely? How do we get to this place? I'm not goin' to cross over that crazy bridge . . . '

Leek pointed out the entrance, and the big man altered his direction. They came through the screening willows into semi-darkness. It was very still and silent with a smell of rottenness that wafted unpleasantly to their nostrils. Mr. Budd sniffed.

'Ugh!' he said, disgustedly. 'The place smells like a graveyard. Rotten an' dank . . . '

'Gloomy kind of hole, ain't it?' remarked Leek, staring about him.

Mr. Budd grunted and led the way to the door of the old building. It was very dark inside and he could see nothing. Pausing on the threshold, he took a box of matches from his pocket and struck a match. In the purple yellow glimmer he caught a glimpse of the great stone roller in the middle, and the flour dust that covered everything with a dirty white film; the rotting sacks that lay huddled against the wall, and something else that was *not* a sack . . .

'Here,' he said, sharply, thrusting the match-box into Leek's hand. 'There's a candle-end over there, two or three of 'em stuck on that stone. Light 'em all, will yer . . .'

The lean sergeant obeyed, and the tiny flames, flickering in the draught, sent distorted, grotesque shadows dancing round the damp walls. Mr. Budd went over to the thing he had seen dimly, sprawling amid the half-filled sacks. Ginger had *not* imagined the terror of the place. She lay on her back, still wearing the camel coat, her hands clenched in a final death agony beside her, her face a blackish-purple and her eyes staring . . .

Mr. Budd stood looking down at this thing which had once been Sandra Brockwell, for nearly a minute, and then he stooped closer, peering at the slender throat. Almost hidden in a fold of the discoloured flesh was a thin cord which had been drawn cruelly tight and tied . . .

'Bin strangled, ain't she?' whispered Leek, joining him.

Mr. Budd nodded.

'Yes,' he muttered. 'Yes . . . ' But his eyes were no longer fixed on the thin cord that had been the means of cutting off life. They had strayed to something that lay on the sacks beside the dead girl. It was a playing-card — the Knave of Diamonds . . .

3

In Superintendent Tidworthy's room, in the police station at Bedlington, a conference took place later on that evening. Major Toppington, Tidworthy himself, and Mr. Budd, all three looking tired and dispirited, faced each other across the small office and tried to decide what line of action they would take next.

After the discovery of Sandra Brockwell's dead body in the old mill, Mr. Budd, leaving the reluctant Leek to guard the place, had gone in search of Dr. Middlesham. The doctor had just come in and listened to what the big man told him in undisguised surprise and horror. After Mr. Budd had telephoned to Bedlington from Middlesham's house and acquainted an equally surprised Tidworthy with the news, he and the doctor had returned to Weeper's Mill, and, in the light of a powerful electric lamp which Middlesham had brought with him, made a closer examination of the place. In the thick mixture of flour dust and mud that covered the floor were a mass of footprints, mostly belonging to Ginger and his friends, to judge from the size, and among them the marks of Sandra's high heels were distinguishable here and there. There were, too, several smudged impressions of a large, square-toed shoe, but none of these was very clear.

Dr. Middlesham reported, after examining the body, that the girl had died from strangulation and had met her death, so far as he could tell, between the hours of eleven and one o'clock on the previous night. It was his opinion that she had been taken completely by surprise for, although there were several scratches on her throat, where she had clawed at the strangling cord, there were no signs of any struggle. It appeared as though the cord had been thrown over her head from behind and drawn tight before she had realized what was happening. And that was all. There was no clue whatever to the identity of the murderer.

Mr. Budd, a greatly depressed and worried man, waited for the arrival of

Superintendent Tidworthy and the police doctor, who confirmed all that Middlesham had said, and then went to The Croft to break the news to Henry Brockwell and his wife. Their reaction to Sandra's death was very much what he had expected. There was no trace of sorrow, only a growing uneasiness most noticeable on the part of Henry. Mr. Budd got the impression that the man was consumed with fear and was trying his best not to show it. Henry Brockwell knew, or guessed, a great deal more than he admitted.

Mr. Budd drove over to Bedlington to attend the conference, which Major Toppington had suggested, without much hope of being able to make any useful contribution to the meeting.

'Well,' remarked the Chief Constable, after he had received an account of this fresh discovery in frowning silence, 'here's the situation as I see it. Two people have been killed within the last month, without the murderer having left a single clue, or without the suggestion of a motive. This second crime bears such a close resemblance to the first that, except for the method of killing, it is almost a repetition. John Brockwell went to keep an unknown appointment in Cooper's Spinney and met his death. Sandra Brockwell kept an equally unknown appointment at Weeper's Mill and also met her death. In each case there was no sign of a struggle, and in each case a card — the Ten of Diamonds in the first instance, and the Knave of Diamonds in the second — was left by the body. These cards may or may not have any real meaning. It is possible that they may have been put there by the murderer purely to confuse the issue . . . '

'No, sir, I don't think so,' put in Mr. Budd, gently. 'I think they were put there for a very real reason — a reason that 'Enry Brockwell knows all about . . . '

'You mean he knows the meaning of these cards?' said the Chief Constable, quickly.

'I'm pretty sure 'e does,' said Mr. Budd, with conviction.

'Then, for the love of heaven, why doesn't he tell us?' exclaimed Superintendent Tidworthy, rubbing the back of his nearly bald head. 'Surely he *wants* the murderer found . . . ?'

'I wouldn't like ter bet on that,' said Mr. Budd, shaking his head. 'I'm not at all sure that 'e *does* want the murderer found.'

Both Major Toppington and the super-intendent stared at him, trying to fully digest the meaning of this astonishing statement.

'But, good heavens, man,' burst out the Chief Constable. 'If he doesn't, why in the world did he badger me to call in Scotland Yard? It was his idea, you know . . . '

'Maybe it was, sir,' said Mr. Budd. 'But I've got a hunch it was for a different reason than what you think . . . '

'What reason?' demanded Tidworthy.

'Protection,' murmured the big man. 'It's my opinion that this feller Brockwell is a badly frightened man. I b'lieve 'e knows who the killer is, an' I believe that he's under the impression that *he'll* get his sooner or later. He was 'opin' that the presence of somebody from Scotland Yard in the dis-trict would scare the murderer off . . . '

'But if he knows who the murderer is, why not tell us?' interrupted Tidworthy.

'That 'ud be the surest way of ensuring his own safety . . . '

'Maybe he dare not,' remarked Mr. Budd, significantly. 'Maybe it 'ud bring somethin' to light that he don't want brought to light . . . '

'You mean something that might land him in gaol?' said Major Toppington.

'Or worse,' said Mr. Budd. 'I think 'e knows the murderer an' the motive for the murders, but 'e dare not say what he knows because it 'ud involve himself up to the neck — an' maybe that's a very good way of puttin' it,' he added, thoughtfully.

The Chief Constable frowned and scratched the side of his face.

'Nothing that was discovered about Brockwell would ever surprise me,' he grunted, after a pause. 'I'm ready to believe that he's capable of anything. But you're suggesting that he's a murderer . . . '

'Or an accessory to a murder,' said Mr. Budd. 'Yes, that's what's in my mind, sir . . . '

'What reason have you for such an idea?' asked Major Toppington.

'Well, now, that's goin' ter be a bit

difficult,' answered Mr. Budd, cautiously. 'It's more of a hunch, if I may put it that way, sir, than somethin' I can produce evidence for . . . '

'But you must have *some* basis for thinking this,' said the Chief Constable, a little impatiently. 'Something must have suggested the idea to you?'

'Oh, yes, sir, somethin' did,' agreed Mr. Budd. 'It was the look on Brockwell's face when I pointed out that the sequence of cards in that queer message was a royal flush in poker. *He* knew the significance of it, an' it frightened 'im.' He rubbed his chin. 'There's several questions I'd like the answers to, sir,' he continued, after a slight pause. 'I'd like ter know the *real* source of all the money Brockwell appears to 'ave — not 'ow 'e *says* he got it, but 'ow he *really* got it. I'd like to know what made 'im come ter live in Long Millford, an' where 'e came *from*. An' I'd like ter know if it's only a coincidence that there are *five* cards in a royal flush in poker an' *five* people in the Brockwell family.'

'It shouldn't be difficult to find answers to your first two questions,' said Major

Toppington. 'Surely a routine inquiry would supply those? But the third . . . Well, what exactly are you getting at?'

'Just this, sir,' replied Mr. Budd, speaking very slowly and distinctly. 'There are five cards in a royal flush, an' we've got two of 'em — the Ten and the Knave of Diamonds. We know what went with 'em. To complete the hand there are three more wanted — the Queen, the King, and the Ace. Are they goin' ter turn up *in similar circumstances?*'

The Chief Constable uttered a sudden, startled ejaculation. Superintendent Tidworthy, who had been staring rather morosely at his blotting-pad, jerked up his bald head and transferred the stare to Mr. Budd.

'You mean . . . You think . . . ?' Major Toppington was slightly incoherent in his astonishment.

'Three more cards an' three more Brockwells,' murmured Mr. Budd, with his eyes almost completely closed. 'Just the right number, ain't it?'

'But . . . but it's fantastic!' stuttered the Chief Constable, completely shaken out

114

of his habitual calm. 'You're suggesting that there are going to be three more murders . . . '

'I think that's the plan, sir,' said Mr. Budd, nodding. 'It's up to us to see that it ain't carried out . . . '

'Sounds a bit far-fetched to me,' grunted Tidworthy. 'Like something out of a book . . . '

'The whole thing is like somethin' out of a book,' said Mr. Budd. 'The first two murders is like somethin' out of a book. I thought so when I first read about 'ow John Brockwell 'ad been killed an' the card pinned to 'is coat, before I was officially connected with the affair at all, an' I still think so. But that don't alter the fact that it's *really* 'appenin'. It only throws a certain amount o' light on the mind of the murderer . . . '

'H'm, I see what you mean.' Major Toppington had succeeded in digesting this new and unexpected angle, and was almost himself again. 'It's your opinion that somebody is trying to wipe out the entire Brockwell family?'

'Yes, sir,' said Mr. Budd. 'That's exac'ly

my opinion . . . '

'Why?' demanded Tidworthy, who was obviously rather sceptical.

The big man shrugged his broad shoulders slightly.

'I can't suggest a reason,' he said. 'Maybe we'll find that out later. And, mark you, I may be altogether wrong. I'm only tellin' you what I *think* . . . '

'I believe there's probably something in your theory, Superintendent,' said the Chief Constable, thoughtfully. 'At least it gives us something to work on. If you're right, then the murderer must be somebody who was connected with Brockwell in the past — before he came to live at Long Millford?'

Mr. Budd nodded.

'Yes, sir, an' pretty closely connected, too,' he said. 'An' somebody who's followed 'im to Long Millford an' is now somewhere in the district 'imself.'

There was a silence. Major Toppington took off his spectacles and polished them vigorously with his handkerchief. Superintendent Tidworthy stared at the dark blue oblong of uncurtained window and drummed gently on the desk with the finger-tips of one hand. Mr. Budd suppressed a large yawn and looked as though he was in imminent danger of falling asleep. He had propounded his theory and, for the moment, had nothing more to say. The Chief Constable replaced his spectacles carefully, put the handkerchief back in his breast pocket, and coughed.

'What line of action do you propose taking, Superintendent?' he asked.

Mr. Budd opened his eyes.

'The most immediate job, sir,' he said, 'is ter prevent the possibility of a repetition — in other words, another murder. What I suggest is this: that Sergeant Leek an' Sergeant Mackleberry take it in turns ter keep a close watch on The Croft an' foller the Brockwells whenever they go anywhere. That is, whenever any one of 'em go out by themselves. There's a good chance this way that, if the murderer tries again, we can catch 'im in the act. In the meanwhile I'll get Scotland Yard to find out all about Brockwell. That may take some time. They'll 'ave to get in touch with the Canadian police to do the job properly.'

The Chief Constable nodded.

'That seems to me to be a very sound scheme,' he agreed. 'What do you think, Tidworthy?'

'It's all right,' said Superintendent Tidworthy, 'always providing, of course, that Budd's idea is right . . .'

'In any case it can't do any harm,' pointed out Mr. Budd.

'You don't think it would do any good to tackle Brockwell?' suggested the Chief Constable. 'Tell him point-blank that we believe that he's holding something back and . . .'

'No, I don't, sir,' broke in Mr. Budd, emphatically. 'I don't think you'd get anythin' out of 'im at all. We've got no evidence that he *does* know anythin', an' he'd only deny it.'

'Perhaps you're right,' said Major Toppington. 'I hope that something comes of it, that's all. I shall be glad to get this business over and done with.'

They discussed the time schedules for the two sergeants and, when these had been settled, the conference broke up.

4

The second 'playing-card murder,' as the newspapers called it, caused something of a sensation. Long Millford, from being a mere point on the map, and hitherto almost unknown, became notorious. Photographs of Weeper's Mill and The Croft were blazoned on the front pages of the national dailies, together with pictures of the dead girl. A horde of reporters descended like locusts on the village, most of them the same men who had been assigned to the first murder; and Mr. Budd, in company with everyone who was even remotely connected with the affair, was subjected to a barrage of questions. The big man was acquainted with the majority of the reporters and liked them. He realized that they had a job of work to do, and so long as it was without prejudice to the police investigation, he was prepared to do all he could to help them. There was one man among them, however, whom he frankly detested. Mr. Joshua Craven was a thin, middle-aged man with a large and drooping nose which always seemed to be appearing where it was least expected or wanted. He was a sour man with a perpetual grievance against his fellow men and the world in general, and was disliked and distrusted by nearly everybody with whom he came in contact. He was attached to no particular newspaper and it was his practice to sell whatever information he succeeded in acquiring to the highest bidder. Anything that was unusual was certain to attract him and he was, as a rule, remarkably successful. The real reason for Lady Hemmingly's divorce was unearthed by Mr. Craven, and he was the only newspaperman to discover it and publish it. The truth behind the broken engagement between Adele Vanisha, the actress, and Lord Doynton was revealed in a caustic article from his rather vitriolic pen; and the right solution to the extraordinary 'chess murder,' which resulted in the suicide of a bishop, came from the same source.

There was no denying that he was a brilliant journalist, but his unpopularity was due to the methods he adopted to get his results. He was utterly and completely unscrupulous and would break his most solemn promise, or betray the closest confidence, with no more compunction than he would drink a cup of tea. Friends to Joshua Craven were merely means to an end and, when this had been achieved, he would drop them as easily as throwing away an empty packet of cigarettes. The red-rimmed, slightly watery eyes that peered short-sightedly through the gold pince-nez missed nothing, and the alert brain was capable of finding a significance in some slight, ordinary little action or word that others passed over.

When Mr. Budd, on his way to the inquest on Sandra Brockwell in the village hall, saw the lean, neatly dressed figure of Mr. Craven strolling along the High Street towards him, his heart sank. The advent of this man meant trouble — trouble and Mr. Craven were synonymous.

'Good morning, Superintendent,' greeted Mr. Craven, halting directly in Mr. Budd's path. 'I was on my way to see you . . . '

'I'm goin' to the inquest,' said Mr. Budd, curtly.

'So am I,' said Mr. Craven. 'Let us walk together.' He turned and fell into step beside Mr. Budd. 'This is a very peculiar and extraordinary case, don't you think? I confess that I am greatly intrigued. What do you suppose lies behind these playing-cards, eh?'

'I don't suppose nothin',' grunted Mr. Budd.

'No? You surprise me.' Mr. Craven pursed his thin lips. 'I should have thought that you would have come to some conclusion. Or perhaps you have and would rather not discuss it? I have only just become interested in the affair. The editor of *Globe News* suggested that I might look into the matter.'

Mr. Budd made no reply. If Mr. Craven thought he was going to work the pump-handle on *him*, he could have another think.

'I understand and respect your caution,' went on the reporter, who respected nothing. 'We are, however, both here for the same reason — to find out the truth.

Perhaps we can be of mutual advantage to each other . . . That's a nice-looking young lady, don't you think?'

Mr. Budd glanced across the street and saw Harriet Lake on the other side.

'A very gifted young lady, too,' continued Mr. Craven, informatively. 'Her name is Miss Harriet Lake and she is an artist. Her father was an artist also — quite a well-known one. Perhaps you've heard of him — Edward Lake. There are three of his pictures in the Academy, and last year there was an exhibition of fifty-seven of them at Leferre Galleries. It was a great pity that he committed suicide . . . '

'Did he?' Mr. Budd was startled out of his silence.

'Didn't you know?' The reporter sounded faintly surprised. 'Dear me, yes. He gassed himself in his studio in Kensington. Let me see, now, that would be the year before last . . . '

'Why?' demanded Mr. Budd. 'What did 'e do it for?'

Mr. Craven looked down his thin, drooping nose.

'Financial reasons,' he answered, vaguely.

'The whole truth of the matter never came out. No,' he repeated, slowly, 'it never came out.'

He managed to convey by his tone that, although the truth had not become public, it was no secret to *him*. Mr. Budd decided that an inquiry concerning the suicide of Edward Lake might prove interesting. Harriet Lake had, and was still, interesting him considerably, though he failed to see how she could be involved in the case. Although the second murder could have conceivably been committed by a woman, the first definitely could not, and there was very little likelihood that two separate people were responsible. Harriet Lake, however, was worth studying, particularly now that there seemed to be something mysterious about her father's death. That there *was* something mysterious about it, he did not question for a moment. Mr. Craven never made mistakes, and his information was always accurate. It had to be, since he made his living by moving through a jungle of latent libel actions, and a mistake would have been fatal.

They had reached the village hall, which was temporarily serving as a court for the coroner, and with a muttered excuse Mr. Budd detached himself from his unwelcome companion and went in search of Superintendent Tidworthy, who was looking after the proceedings. The small hall was very full. The inquest had provided an irresistible attraction. The Coroner, a fussy little solicitor from Bedlington, was sorting his papers at his table, rather nervous and ill-at-ease at the presence of so many reporters, and the hall was filled with a muted buzz from small groups of people who were whispering to each other excitedly. The three remaining members of the Brock-well family were standing by the wall, staring rather sullenly and resentfully, and looking as though they were very annoyed with the whole proceedings, as very probably they were.

'I've seen the Coroner,' whispered Tidworthy, when Mr. Budd joined him, 'and he has agreed to keep the proceedings as short as possible. After the evidence of the cause of death, we shall ask for an adjournment . . . '

'Who are those people?' interrupted Mr. Budd, nodding towards the back of the hall. 'Near that window by the door?'

Superintendent Tidworthy, rather annoyed at the interruption, looked across.

'Sir Oswald and Lady Pipp-Partington,' he answered.

'Oh, they are, are they?' murmured Mr. Budd, eyeing them with interest. 'Um!'

Tidworthy seemed to be a trifle surprised at this noncommittal comment, but he said nothing. Mr. Budd continued to gaze speculatively at the two people who had attracted his attention. Sir Oswald Pipp-Partington was a tall, lean man, approaching sixty, with almost snow-white hair. His face, rather lined, was of a healthy tan, and he evidently spent much of his time in the open air. Lady Pipp-Partington was an older replica of her daughter, Clarissa. The big man looked around expecting to see her there, too, but there was no sign of her. Doctor Middlesham was there, however, and with him was a pretty, fair-haired woman whom Mr. Budd guessed, from a certain facial resemblance, to be

126

his sister, Rita. He liked the look of the Pipp-Partingtons. They were the real thing, he thought, something that is born and not made. Only generations of good breeding could produce that type . . .

The Coroner rapped on his table with a gavel; there was a sudden complete hush, and then, rather nervously, he opened the proceedings. After a short preliminary speech, Henry Brockwell was called to the stand and identified the body of the deceased as that of his daughter, Sandra. He was followed by a half-frightened and half-proud Ginger who related, with sundry pauses, how he had come to discover the body at Weeper's Mill. There was a certain amount of laughter, instantly suppressed by the indignant Coroner, when he haltingly described the reason for his presence at the Mill and mentioned the contemplated initiation of Tommy Potts into the 'Hawks.'

Tommy Potts' father, who was a member of the jury, grinned broadly at the reference to his son. When Ginger was dismissed, reluctantly (for he was just beginning to enjoy this novel position) his place was taken by Doctor Middlesham, who briefly described the cause of death and the time at which, in his opinion, it had taken place. Doctor Wakefield followed him and confirmed everything he had said. Henry Brockwell was then recalled and testified to what he knew of his daughter's movements on the evening of her death. Tom Custer, looking very self-conscious and not a little suspicious, as though he fully expected the witness-stand to turn suddenly into a dock and the Coroner to give him a stiff sentence, related how he had seen the dead girl leave the house, described what she had been wearing, and the time by the clock when she had passed him in the hall. The last witness was Superintendent Tidworthy. He gave a very brief account of how he had been notified of the discovery at Weeper's Mill, and what he had found on his arrival, and wound up his evidence with a request for an adjournment. This request the Coroner immediately granted, and the short proceedings were concluded. To the majority present it was very disappointing. They had hoped, at least, to hear what Scotland Yard had to say about it; but, at his own wish, Mr. Budd had not been called, preferring that Tidworthy should represent the police.

On the way out the big man suddenly found Mr. Joshua Craven once more at his side.

'Not very helpful or illuminating, was it?' remarked the reporter, looking at him sidewise. 'Have the police got something up their sleeves, or are they completely baffled?'

'S'pose you wait and see?' grunted Mr. Budd, not very politely.

'I shall,' replied Mr. Craven. 'I shall most certainly wait *and* see. By the way, have you seen or heard anything of a man called Roger Naylor? No? Dear me, that rather surprises me. I think you will — yes, I'm quite *sure* you will . . . '

He nodded amiably and drifted away.

5

Mr. Budd ate the substantial lunch provided for him at the Peal o' Bells without enjoyment. He was feeling frustrated and, in consequence, irritable. He had sent in his request to Scotland Yard for particulars concerning Henry Brockwell's past history and had instituted the watch on The Croft, which he had suggested at the Chief Constable's conference, and now there seemed nothing more he could do but await results. In no other case that he could remember was there such a complete absence of clues. The murderer had struck twice and left nothing behind that might lead to his identity. Mr. Budd remembered his somewhat caustic comments about the inability of the local police to have discovered anything essential after three weeks' investigation and realized, now, that he had done them an injustice. Here he was, himself, in very much the same position. It was true that he had found a fresh angle on the affair, but there was no guarantee that it was the right one. It was all very well to evolve fantastic theories, but quite another matter to substantiate them.

If he was right and the unknown killer *did* try to repeat his performance with another member of the Brockwell family, there was every chance that he would be caught. But would he? *Did* the plan embrace the elimination of *all* the Brockwells? If it didn't, then Leek and Mackleberry were wasting their time, and so was he for that matter. Yet the more he pondered on the subject, the more convinced he became that his idea was the right one. Unless, of course, it was just what the murderer wished the police to think. That was a possible explanation for the playing-cards and the message — a kind of elaborate red-herring that the murderer had dragged across the scent. If this were the case, then the murders would cease with Sandra, for the killer would have completed his plan. In this case, too, he — Mr. Budd — would have to look for a different motive — a much simpler one. Perhaps that *was* it, after all. Perhaps he was allowing all the trimmings to blind him to what might be nothing but a very ordinary crime — a dual murder for revenge or jealousy or both. The vast majority of murders were committed for very simple motives — totally inadequate motives for the most part, except to the warped mind of the murderer. Was this one of basic simplicity in which the playing-cards and the rest of it had been added to distract the attention — like a conjuror's patter? Mr. Budd recollected the expression on Henry Brockwell's face when he had mentioned that the list of cards in the message made a royal flush in poker, and shook his head. They *had* meant something to *him* — something that was frightening . . .

The big man finished his lunch and went up to his room for a wash. As he laved his face in the basin, his mind came back to the advent of Joshua Craven. That clever and cunning reporter seemed to know a great deal more about the case than he did. Why had he brought up the subject of Edward Lake's suicide and hinted that there were mysterious circumstances surrounding it, and what had he meant by his final reference to a Roger Naylor? Very definitely he knew something — most likely he had been quietly working on the case ever since the murder of John Brockwell. But what had Edward Lake's suicide and the unknown Roger Taylor to do with that? Craven appeared to think that there was a link, but how had he stumbled on it? Probably during the amassing of the curious and out-of-the-way information which was so essential to his particular type of work. The murder of John Brockwell had become connected in his mind with something he had previously discovered about Edward Lake and this man Naylor. That *must* be it.

Mr. Budd lit a cigar and lay down on the bed. A brief, ruminative rest, he thought, and he would take advantage of Harriet Lake's invitation. Maybe he would learn something.

At three o'clock he got up, washed his hands and brushed his hair, and went downstairs. Mr. Duffy was in the bar, leisurely wiping glasses, and the stout superintendent inquired the nearest way to Mill Lane. The landlord directed him clearly and concisely and he set forth to find Harriet Lake's cottage. It was a lovely afternoon, full of the scents of May, but there were signs in the sky that the spell of fine weather was drawing to a close. The drifts of speckled clouds that were forming suggested wind and, with it, probably rain.

Mill Lane proved to be a lane in actual fact. It wound its way between green hedgerows and under overhanging trees, heavy with hawthorn blossom, which filled the air with perfume. There was no sign of anything in the nature of a cottage at first, but presently, rounding a bend, Mr. Budd came in sight of it. It was a pretty place of white, creeper-covered stone, and larger than he had expected. He saw when he got nearer that it was, in reality, two cottages which had been converted into one. The garden beyond the gate was neat and full of old-world flowers that dotted the beds in fresh green clumps, giving promise of the profusion of bloom that the summer would bring. There were a number of standard roses: sturdy, well-established trees with thick bushy heads; and he noted with approval — for he was a great expert on roses — that they had all been carefully and properly pruned. Behind the cottage he caught a glimpse of a wide lawn and the hint of an orchard, and he sighed as he walked up the path to the porch. Here was a place where one could live in peace and happiness, forgetting all the sordidness and pettiness, the greed and cruelty that men ironically called civilization. This was the sort of spot he would like to retire to, spending the rest of his days among his beloved roses, with a little pleasant company now and again from the inhabitants of the village and an evening or two at the Peal o' Bells . . .

He raised his hand and knocked with the iron knocker at the door. There was a slight pause and then he heard footsteps, and the door opened. Harriet Lake, wearing a loose kind of smock and carrying a palette and brushes, looked at him.

'Good afternoon, miss,' said Mr. Budd, raising his hat. 'I thought I'd come along and 'ave that cup o' tea you mentioned, but if you're busy don't worry about . . . '

'Come in,' said Harriet, opening the door wider. 'You've timed it very well. I've just put the kettle on.'

She led the way into a large, airy room, obviously made from two smaller rooms by the removal of the dividing wall. The furniture was old and good, and by the north window was a large easel holding an unfinished picture on which Harriet Lake had evidently been working when she had been disturbed by his knock. It was a conventional set piece — a bowl of roses on a mahogany table — but even Mr. Budd, whose knowledge of art would have barely covered a postage stamp, could see that there was something about it that lifted it out of the ordinary. The roses were of a colour that no living roses had ever achieved, and the table was queerly distorted, but the whole glowed and quivered with life.

'Sit down and make yourself comfortable,' said Harriet, putting her palette and brushes down on a table near the easel that was littered with paints and bottles and jars of brushes. 'That settee may not look very comfortable, but I can assure you that it is.'

Mr. Budd laid his hat down on the floor and tried the settee. It was very comfortable indeed.

'I thought detectives never took their hats off?' remarked Harriet, quizzically.

'Some of 'em don't,' said Mr. Budd. 'Maybe I'm not a very good detective. You've got a nice place 'ere, miss.'

'It is nice, isn't it?' she said. 'I think I can hear the kettle boiling. Excuse me a moment.' She hurried away, and settling himself comfortably in a corner of the settee, the big man took stock of his surroundings. Very nice indeed, he thought approvingly. There was not much furniture, but what there was was right. The floor was of oak, darkened by age and much polishing, and there were Persian rugs of soft colours. A restful, pleasant atmosphere permeated the place, like the subtle fragrance from an old bowl of potpourri. Mr. Budd contrasted this cottage with the ornate house of the Brockwells to the latter's disadvantage. Here was taste and comfort; there only lavishness and display.

Harriet Lake came back with a laden tray, which she set down on a low table near the settee.

'You know,' she said, as she busied herself pouring out the tea, 'I wondered whether you would come. I rather thought you would, but I wasn't sure.' She handed him a cup of tea. 'Help yourself to sugar,' she went on, 'and try some of those sandwiches, or the cakes. I made the cakes myself . . . ' She helped herself to a sandwich and sat back nibbling at it and regarding him steadily.

'I suppose it was curiosity,' she remarked, suddenly.

'What was curiosity, miss?' he asked.

'That brought you,' she said. 'I rather expected you would come when I saw you with that man this morning.'

'D'you mean Craven?' he inquired, and she nodded.

'You know very well who I mean,' she retorted. 'What's he doing here?'

Mr. Budd finished a mouthful of sandwich.

'He's here to find out all about the murders, miss,' he answered. ''E's been commissioned by the *Globe News*. Do you know 'im?'

'Of course I do — and you know that I do,' she said, impatiently. 'He's told you all about Father, hasn't he?'

'Well, he *did* mention your father, miss,' admitted Mr. Budd, cautiously.

'I was sure he did,' she said. 'And that's why you're here, isn't it?'

'No, miss,' said Mr. Budd, truthfully. 'Not altogether it ain't. I'd made up me mind to come before I saw Craven . . . '

'What did he tell you?' she demanded, and then before he could reply: 'It doesn't matter. I'll tell you the truth. It will save you a great deal of trouble and me a great deal of annoyance. Have another sandwich?'

'Thank you, miss,' said Mr. Budd, and he took one.

'My father,' said Harriet, speaking very quickly and without any variation in the tone of her voice, 'committed suicide. He killed himself because he got into a financial difficulty from which he couldn't extricate himself. And the man who got him into it was Henry Brockwell.' She saw the startled look on Mr. Budd's rather bovine face and smiled. It was a hard, mirthless smile, which only touched her mouth. 'That surprises you, does it?' she went on. 'Well, it's the truth and I told you I was going to tell you the truth. Henry Brockwell ruined my father and was just as much responsible for his death as if he'd killed him. Now you know why I hate him and all his wretched brood . . . '

'You didn't have to tell me this, miss,' began Mr. Budd.

'I know I didn't,' she broke in, curtly. 'But I prefer it that way. I told you before that I hate questions and spying and probing. I'd rather explain anything of my own free will than have it dragged out of me.'

'Well, I can understand that attitude, miss,' said Mr. Budd. 'I'm rather like that myself. Would you care to tell me 'ow Brockwell got your father into a mess?'

She nodded.

'My father was quite a well-known

painter,' she said. 'He made a good bit of money from his pictures, at least it was a good bit to him. But in his early days he'd had a very bad time and sometimes gone for days without food. The memory of that time was always with him. He had a horror that something might happen to bring it all back again. It was almost an obsession with him, and to add to it his eyesight was failing him. He'd saved about three thousand pounds, but if anything happened to stop him working this would soon dwindle to nothing and once more poverty would be knocking at the door. Almost to the exclusion of everything else, his mind was occupied with schemes for a permanent financial security.

It was round about this time that he met Henry Brockwell. How he met him, or where he met him, I don't know, and it doesn't really matter. Brockwell was planning a big deal in timber — I don't know all the details of it, and that doesn't matter, either. All that matters is that he persuaded father to invest every penny of his savings, holding out as a bait that they would be trebled in a few months.

Something went wrong — a concession from the Canadian government was refused, I believe — and Father lost everything. The whole thing, in my opinion, was a swindle engineered by Brockwell because he saw an easy way of pocketing three thousand pounds. Now you can understand why I hate him and his blasted family. I expect there are hundreds of people who feel the same as I do, because I should imagine that's how he's made his money . . . Have some more tea?'

Mr. Budd held out his empty cup and she took it.

'Thank you, miss,' he said. 'Yes, I can understand 'ow you feel about Brockwell . . . '

'But don't start thinking that *I* had anything to do with the murders,' warned Harriet, busy with the teapot. 'I didn't.'

'I wasn't thinkin' anythin' like that,' murmured the big man. 'May I 'ave a cake? Thank you.' He helped himself. 'Did you meet this feller, Brockwell, yourself?'

'Once,' she nodded. 'Father brought

him to the studio in Kensington. I didn't like him . . . ' She broke off as there came a knock on the front door.

'Who can that be?' she said, frowning. 'Excuse me, will you?'

She got up and went out. Mr. Budd, munching his cake, heard the door open and her exclamation: 'I didn't expect you . . . ' The deep voice of a man rumbled something and then Harriet said: 'Well, you'd better come in . . . '

She entered the room, followed by a man whose huge size filled the doorway.

'This is Superintendent Budd of Scotland Yard,' she said. 'He's investigating the murders . . . Mr. Budd, this a friend of mine, Mr. Roger Naylor.'

6

It took quite a lot to surprise Mr. Budd, but he was surprised then. It flashed across his mind that as a first-class prophet, Joshua Craven would take a lot of beating. He had said that morning that he would meet Roger Naylor and here *was* Roger Naylor very much in the flesh. It was incredible. Mr. Naylor was exceptionally good-looking and quite one of the largest young men the stout superintendent had ever seen. It wasn't that he was fat. It was doubtful if he had an ounce of super-fluous flesh on his bones. It was just that in every way he was big — a broad-shouldered, towering giant of a man, with an unruly mop of curly fair hair. Mr. Budd pulled himself together sufficiently to offer a conventional greeting.

'Sit down, Roger,' invited Harriet. 'Will you have some tea?'

Mr. Naylor stammered, rather diffi-dently, that he would. It was easy to see that his size did not carry with it a corresponding confidence. He was almost painfully shy and nervous. He perched himself on a totally inadequate chair and fidgeted uneasily.

'What brought you over from Bedlington?' asked Harriet, pouring out tea. *Had* she expected another visitor? thought Mr. Budd, or was it an accident that there happened to be a spare cup and saucer?

'I — I came over to see *you*,' answered Roger Naylor. 'I thought — er — perhaps you'd like to come to a film tonight. There's a pretty good one, I'm told, at the Rialto . . . '

'That's very sweet of you, Roger,' she said, giving him his tea. 'I think I would, rather.'

But I'll bet that isn't what you came for, thought Mr. Budd. You thought that up on the spur of the moment. And why has the girl gone suddenly all uneasy? There's something funny here.

But if there *was* anything funny, neither Naylor nor Harriet Lake were giving it away. They carried on a spasmodic and desultory conversation about the more ordinary subjects, into which they dragged Mr. Budd. The talk fluctuated from gardening to politics until the big man, feeling that he could no longer stretch his already protracted visit, reluctantly took his leave. Harriet Lake came with him to the door and he was sure that there was relief on her face.

As he walked slowly back to the Peal o' Bells, Mr. Budd mentally chewed over his afternoon. Who *was* Roger Naylor? Someone of importance in this queer business he was investigating or Joshua Craven would not have mentioned him. It was queer that that unpleasant man should have been so *certain* that he and Naylor would meet. Why had he? That was known only to himself and was likely to remain so. But he must have had some object in calling attention to Naylor at all. Craven was not the type of man to be gratuitously helpful unless it was going to prove of advantage to himself. For some unknown reason he had wished to draw Mr. Budd's attention to Harriet Lake and Roger Naylor. It was very strange and it made the big man feel as though he were being used as a kind of stooge — a remarkably uncomfortable feeling and one that he found very irritating.

When he reached the Peal o' Bells he found, to his surprise, that a note had been left for him during his absence.

'It's from Sir Oswald Pipp-Partington, sir,' said Mr. Duffy, openly curious. ''Ancock, the chauffeur, brought it just after you'd gone out.'

Mr. Budd, as curious as Mr. Duffy, ripped open the envelope. The note was very brief. Would Superintendent Budd kindly call at his earliest convenience?

The big man pocketed the letter and pursed his thick lips. Why should Sir Oswald Pipp-Partington wish to see him? He decided to find out without delay, although he was feeling tired, and inquired the way to Millford Lodge. Mr. Duffy directed him, and Mr. Budd, after a hurried wash and brush-up, set forth to discover for what reason he had been sent for.

Millford Lodge was, he found, after a quarter of an hour's walk, a delightful old house standing in about four acres of ground which extended to within a few hundred yards of Cooper's Spinney. It was not a large house. He concluded that at one time it had probably been in actual fact the lodge to a larger house — most likely The Croft, which Clarissa had said had once been the home of the Pipp-Partingtons. In answer to his knock the door was opened by a very old man in the correct, but shabby, black garb of an upper servant. He ushered Mr. Budd into a small room off the hall and went to acquaint his master of his arrival. It was quite obvious, thought the stout superintendent, that the Pipp-Partingtons were not well-off. The carpets were old and threadbare, and the room into which he had been shown required quite a number of minor repairs.

After a short interval the elderly servant came back and conducted him into a larger room that was lined with books and was evidently a kind of combined library and study. Sir Oswald Pipp-Partington, who was looking out of the window, turned as he was announced.

'Come in, Superintendent,' he said, in a pleasant voice. 'It was good of you to come so speedily in answer to my request. Can I offer you any refreshment?'

'Thank you, sir,' said Mr. Budd, gratefully. 'If you should happen to 'ave any beer . . . '

'Bring a bottle of ale and the sherry, Flower,' ordered Sir Oswald, and the old man bowed and withdrew.

'I've no doubt,' continued his master, 'that you are wondering why I should have asked you to come and see me?'

'Well, yes, sir, I am,' agreed Mr. Budd.

'It is rather a delicate matter,' said Sir Oswald, passing a nervous hand over his mouth. 'It has taken me a long time to decide whether I ought to mention it. Please sit down.'

Mr. Budd lowered himself into a shabby leather chair and waited, wondering what was coming. This old aristocrat was nervous and undecided and he wondered what the reason could be. Sir Oswald fidgeted with some books on the flat-topped writing-table and seemed to be making up his mind how to begin. Flower returned with a tray of glasses, a large bottle of beer, and a decanter of sherry. He poured out a glass of beer for Mr. Budd and sherry for his master, and once again withdrew.

Sir Oswald produced a box of cigars and offered it to the stout detective. Mr. Budd took one and thanked him, though he would infinitely have preferred one of his own evil-smelling black atrocities. Sir Oswald courteously supplied him with a light and took a sip of his sherry.

'What I wish to speak about,' he said, slowly, and with an apparent reluctance, 'concerns, or I should say, *may* concern these terrible murders . . . ' He stopped and frowned at his glass.

'Yes, sir?' murmured Mr. Budd, encouragingly. 'You have some information that may help us?'

Sir Oswald Pipp-Partington nodded.

'I think so,' he said. 'Of course, it may not have anything to do with the murders at all. I cannot be sure . . . '

'Suppose, sir,' suggested the big man, as the other seemed in danger of drifting into silence, 'that you tell me what it is and leave *me* to see about that?'

'Yes, yes,' agreed Sir Oswald. 'That is

my intention. I was considering how best to state the matter. It was on the night when this unfortunate woman — er — Sandra Brockwell, met her death. I had occasion to be out rather later than is my wont and I saw the — er — woman talking to a man . . . '

'You did, sir?' said Mr. Budd, with interest. 'What time was this?'

'About a quarter past eleven,' answered Sir Oswald. 'They were standing at the entrance to Willow Lane which, as you know, leads to the old mill. I have hesitated to mention this before, because the man is a tenant of mine and I cannot imagine that he could have any guilty knowledge . . . '

'You mean you know this man who was with her, sir?' broke in Mr. Budd.

'Yes.' Sir Oswald looked very distressed and worried. 'Yes. There was a moon, you remember? The man was Charles Antrim.'

7

This, thought Mr. Budd, is evidently my day for being surprised. This is the second within a few hours. Antrim was the farmer from whom the pitchfork which had killed John Brockwell was alleged to have been stolen. And he had been in the company of Sandra a short while before she had met her death . . .

'I cannot believe,' said Sir Oswald Pipp-Partington, shaking his head, 'that Antrim can be involved in the tragic death of this girl. He's a very steady, hardworking young fellow, and his family have had the farm for years . . . '

'All the same, sir,' said Mr. Budd, 'it's a queer coincidence that the weapon which killed John Brockwell came from 'is farm. And then again, why 'asn't he come forward an' said that 'e saw Miss Brockwell on the night she was killed . . . ?'

'I think that is understandable,' interrupted Sir Oswald, quickly. 'If he should have met her by accident, it would be natural that he might be afraid of arousing suspicion against himself if he mentioned the matter. It is quite understandable that he should keep it to himself . . . '

'I s'pose 'e might look at it that way,' conceded Mr. Budd, and he took a long drink from his glass. 'Was 'e friendly with Miss Brockwell, d'you know, sir?'

'That I could not tell you,' answered Sir Oswald. 'They appeared to be arguing when I saw them.'

'Did they see you, sir?' inquired the big man.

'No. I was hidden from their view by a hedge . . . '

'But you are quite certain that the man was Antrim?'

'Yes, unfortunately I am quite certain about that.'

'H'm,' murmured Mr. Budd. 'It seems to me rather late for a farmer to be out, don't you think, sir?'

'As a matter of fact it struck *me* as odd,' agreed Sir Oswald. He lifted his glass and drained the remainder of his sherry. 'Can I offer you some more ale, Superintendent?'

'No, thank you, sir.' Mr. Budd got heavily to his feet. 'I'm very much obliged to you for the information.'

'I sincerely hope that it won't lead to any sort of trouble for Antrim,' said Sir Oswald. 'I was most reluctant to have to mention it. It was a case of inclination versus duty and duty won . . . '

He accompanied Mr. Budd to the front door.

'A bad lot, these Brockwells,' he remarked, suddenly, as the fat detective was taking his leave. 'Bad altogether . . . '

It was remarkable, thought Mr. Budd, as he waddled down the drive, how everybody in Long Millford seemed to dislike the Brockwells. It was unanimous. Up to now he had not discovered anyone who had said a good word for them. Their presence was regarded rather as a plague might have been.

As he made his way in the direction of Antrim's farm, Mr. Budd found plenty to occupy his mind. It was, to say the least of it, very peculiar that Charles Antrim should have been talking to Sandra Brockwell on that night and at that time. It almost looked as though *he* was the reason for her going out. If so, then there must have been an appointment. It was very significant because it seemed scarcely likely that the girl would have had *two* appointments so late at night; and, if she had had only *one*, and that with Antrim, then it was only plausible to suppose that Antrim was the murderer. In which case he was almost certainly the murderer of John, too. There was, of course, the alternative that Sandra, on her way to keep an appointment with the murderer, had met Antrim by accident, though it seemed rather strange that he should have been out at such a late hour. The entire village, being mostly land workers and farm labourers, was in bed and asleep soon after nine. And then it suddenly occurred to him that it was also strange that Sir Oswald Pipp-Partington had been abroad so late . . . Quite a lot of strange things that day to think about, small things mostly; nothing that really pointed to a solution of the problem . . .

He came at last to Antrim's farm. It was a big, rambling place, but was tidy and well kept. To reach the house he had to pass through a yard in which two motor tractors stood under a lean-to shed, and they were almost new. Charles Antrim was up-to-date and apparently fairly prosperous. Mr. Budd found the entrance to the farmhouse and knocked.

A woman came to the door; a stout, rosy-cheeked woman with white hair.

'Good evenin', ma'am,' said Mr. Budd. 'Could I 'ave a word with Mr. Charles Antrim?'

'I should think you could,' said the white-haired woman, cheerfully, and turning her head she called: 'Charlie! Here's someone wants to see you.'

'Who is it, mother?' answered a voice from somewhere within.

'I don't know — you'd better come and see,' said Mrs. Antrim.

There was a slight pause and then a man appeared. He was tall and dark, fairly good-looking in a very ordinary way, and aged about thirty.

'You want to see me?' he asked, looking

interrogatively at the big man.

'Yes, sir,' said Mr. Budd. 'That is if you are Mr. Charles Antrim?'

'I'm Charles Antrim. What do you want?' said the man.

Mr. Budd introduced himself.

'I should like to ask you one or two questions,' he said, and he saw a look of uneasiness come into the other's eyes.

'You'd better come in,' said Antrim, shortly, and he led the way into a sitting-room full of old-fashioned furniture and bric-a-brac. 'Now,' he went on, facing the stout man, 'what is it you wanted to ask me?'

'I'm given to understand that you was a friend of Miss Sandra Brockwell's,' said Mr. Budd. 'Is that right?'

'I knew her — yes,' answered Antrim, after a momentary hesitation.

'When did you last see her?' asked Mr. Budd.

Antrim frowned, pursed his lips, and looked up at the low ceiling.

'I'm not quite sure,' he replied. 'Not exactly . . . '

'Maybe I can help you to remember,' murmured Mr. Budd. 'Wasn't it on the night she was killed?'

Mrs. Antrim, who had followed her son into the parlour, gave a queer, choked little gasp and the rosiness fled from her cheeks.

'No,' she said, sharply. 'No . . . '

'Don't be in a 'urry to answer,' said Mr. Budd, softly. 'Just think it over carefully . . . '

'There's no need,' broke in Antrim, curtly. 'I *did* see her that night, but only for a few minutes . . . '

'Charlie!' cried his mother, fearfully. 'What are you saying . . . ?'

'It's all right, mother,' he said, gently. 'I've got no reason to hide anything . . . '

'You never told me,' she said, with a catch in her voice. 'You never told me . . . '

'I never told anybody,' he said. 'I didn't see any point in telling anybody . . . '

'What time was it that you saw Miss Brockwell?' asked Mr. Budd.

'I don't know the exact time — round about a quarter past eleven, I think,' answered Antrim.

'Did you meet her by appointment?'

inquired the big man.

'No.' Charles Antrim snapped out the negative almost before he had finished putting the question.

'It was in Willow Lane that you saw her, wasn't it?' It was more of a statement than a question. 'An' you met 'er there by accident, is that it?'

'Yes, that's it,' agreed Antrim, playing nervously with a vase.

'Are you usually out so late, Mr. Antrim?' said Mr. Budd.

Antrim shook his head.

'No,' he replied. 'But that night I couldn't sleep. I'd had a tiring day and I'd gone to bed early, but I couldn't sleep. So I got up and went for a walk. I was coming back down Willow Lane when I met San . . . Miss Brockwell . . . '

Mr. Budd noted the quickly rectified slip, but he made no comment — then.

'You met Miss Brockwell?' he repeated. 'Weren't you surprised to see her at that hour?'

'A little,' admitted Antrim. 'Not as much as I should have been if it had been anyone else.'

'I see,' remarked Mr. Budd. 'And you stopped and spoke to her? Did she say why she was there or where she was goin'?'

'No.'

'How long did you stay talkin' to her?'

'Not very long ... I couldn't say exactly.'

'It wasn't a friendly talk, was it?' said Mr. Budd. 'You 'ad a bit of an argument, didn't you?'

'How do you know all this?' demanded Antrim, angrily. 'Were you spying on us?'

Mr. Budd shook his head.

'If I 'ad been, I shouldn't be askin' you to tell me what 'appened,' he said, reasonably. 'What was this argument about?'

'It was a purely personal matter,' said Antrim, 'and nobody's business but mine and Miss Brockwell's ... '

'Miss Brockwell ain't got any business,' interrupted Mr. Budd. 'A short while after you was arguing with her she was strangled ... '

'I had nothing to do with that,' cried Antrim. 'Good God, you don't think it

160

was *me*, do you?'

'It was *somebody*,' said Mr. Budd, 'an' so far you're the only person we *know* she met that night . . . '

'Oh, no, no!' exclaimed Mrs. Antrim, in a horrified whisper.

'Be quiet, mother,' said Antrim, gently, and then to Mr. Budd: 'Yes, I suppose I am. But I can assure you there *must* have been someone else — someone she was on her way to see when I met her . . . '

'Did she say anythin' that led you to suppose that?' asked Mr. Budd.

'Well, yes, in a way she did.' Antrim hesitated, and then continued with a rush, as though if he didn't speak very quickly he might change his mind and not speak at all: 'Look here, I suppose I'd better tell you all about it. It's not a thing I want to talk about to anyone, but it's the only way to make you understand. Sandra and I were at one time very good friends . . . I thought that I was in love with her. What it really was was a passing infatuation, but I didn't realize it at the time. She made me think that she was fond of me . . . We used to meet several nights a week — at the corner of Willow Lane. After a month or two she began to break the appointments. She made the excuse that she couldn't get out, but I guessed that she was beginning to get fed-up, or had found someone else.

Once, when she should have met me and didn't, I saw her get out of a car at the gate of The Croft and the next time we met and she started the old excuse I told her that she was lying. She flared up into a rage and we had a violent row.' Antrim's voice took on a bitter tone. 'She told me just what she thought of me and what she'd always thought of me. I'd been an amusing stopgap while she was looking round for someone more exciting . . . It was all rather sordid and I realized what a fool I'd been. But, I don't know whether you will understand what I mean. Although I was no longer in love with her, I hated the idea of her giving me the chuck like this for somebody else. I think a lot of it was pride, but there was a good deal of jealousy about it as well . . . I can't really explain in words *what* it was, but it made me determined, after that night, to find out *who* the man was Sandra had taken up with.

I used to hang about The Croft waiting for her to come out, and several times I saw her meet somebody in a car, but I could never see who it was. And then one night — the night you're asking me about — I saw her leave The Croft and I followed her, hoping that she was going to meet this unknown man. She must have known that I was following her, because when I turned the corner into Willow Lane she had stopped and was waiting for me. She was in a raging temper and I wasn't exactly calm. There was a flaming row. She said if I didn't stop spying on her she'd inform the police. That it was none of my business what she did, or where she went, or who she saw. After a few minutes of this sort of thing I told her she wasn't worth bothering about, anyway, and flung off in a rage . . . And that's all.'

Mr. Budd gently rubbed his many chins. Antrim's story was plausible, but was it the truth? Had he left Sandra Brockwell at the end of Willow Lane or had he . . . ?

'You don't know what 'appened to 'er after that?' he said, breaking into his own thoughts.

Antrim shook his head.

'No,' he declared. 'I was so angry that I never even looked back . . .'

'I always told you no good would come of knowing that girl,' broke in Mrs. Antrim. 'A bad lot if ever there was one. I don't know why you ever got mixed up with her . . .'

'Because I was a fool,' replied her son, bitterly. 'I've admitted that, haven't I?'

'It's a good thing you found it out before it was too late,' said Mrs. Antrim.

Yes, but had he, thought Mr. Budd. Had those strong, well-shaped hands pulled that strangling cord round the girl's throat and tied it? There was motive enough — and opportunity. A man in a jealous rage was capable of anything. But what about the card — the Knave of Diamonds? Had that just been a blind — put there to make it look as though the murder was the work of the same person who had killed John? Would Antrim have been clever and cool enough to have thought of a thing like that? The big man was undecided. If this infatuated young farmer *had* killed Sandra, then all his theories came tumbling heavily to the ground ... No, there was something more to it than that — a lot more ...

He put several further questions to Antrim, but was unable to shake his story. The last he had seen of Sandra Brockwell was her standing at the entrance to Willow Lane ...

Mr. Budd walked slowly back to the Peal o' Bells. He was very tired, for he had covered more ground that day than was usual with him. He was not fond of physical exercise if it could be avoided and his feet and legs ached. The wind had risen and it was colder. Ugly-looking black clouds were gathering on the horizon and there was that unmistakable tang in the air which usually heralded rain. There was every sign that it would be a wet night and he thought of Leek. It was the lean sergeant's turn for duty at The Croft that night — an unenviable job at the best of times, but thoroughly unpleasant in the rain ... Was he wasting his time? Had the murderer finished with Sandra, or was he planning to strike again? Mr. Budd sighed wearily. They could only wait and see . . .

8

The rain began to fall just before midnight. It was gentle at first, but very soon developed into a downpour, with a gusty wind that blew the heavy drops into the face of Sergeant Leek as he set forth from Mrs. Cutts's cottage to relieve Sergeant Mackleberry, who had been keeping a steadfast vigil at The Croft for four hours. That was the arrangement. Four hours each. Leek would take Mackleberry's place until four o'clock and then Mackleberry would come back and carry on until eight o'clock in the morning. There was no watch kept during the day. Mr. Budd had not considered that it was worthwhile — from eight in the evening to eight in the morning was, in his opinion, sufficient. The murderer, if he tried again, would try during the hours of darkness. This meant that every alternate night one of them did eight hours, split into two periods of four hours each. Tomorrow it would be Leek's turn to watch that dreadful house, to which even the moonlight could not give a semblance of beauty, from eight to twelve and again from four to eight. Curiously enough, he preferred that duty to the four hours in the middle of the night.

Sergeant Mackleberry had nothing to report. Mr. Custer had appeared at a few minutes after nine and walked down to the village to post a letter. He had carried a letter in his hand when he had left the house and had not been carrying it when he returned, so the sergeant concluded that that had been the reason for his brief excursion. He was indoors again at half-past nine. And that was all. Nobody else had either come or gone.

Sergeant Leek was not surprised. The whole thing, in his opinion, was a waste of time that might be more profitably spent in bed. He imparted this conviction to Sergeant Mackleberry in no uncertain terms. Mackleberry was not altogether inclined to agree with him, but he was a cautious man who preferred to compromise whenever it was possible, and refused to be drawn into making a direct statement either way.

When he had gone, the disgruntled Leek pulled his shabby mackintosh closer round his bony form and settled down to four hours of resigned misery. There was a patch of woodland facing the gate to The Croft from which he and Mackleberry had decided, from the beginning, to conduct their vigil. It was a very small patch, but a very dense one, and it commanded not only a clear view of the gate, but of the drive and the front door of the house as well. To-night it was a very wet and cold patch. Every time the gusts of wind shook the trees and bushes, Leek was deluged by the accumulated raindrops. A miserable and uncomfortable way of spending half the night, he thought disgustedly. And all to no purpose. At least not up to now, anyway, and goodness knew how long it might have to go on before anything happened, if it *ever* did.

Old Budd got some queer ideas in that fat head of his at times, and they nearly always involved him, Leek, in some unpleasant job. And the trouble was that he nearly always turned out to be right. Well, he hoped he'd be right in this case. A bit of excitement would be welcome — anything would be welcome to break the monotony of standing in the middle of a damp thicket for hours and feeling your legs gradually get number and number. It was a wonder that he hadn't caught pneumonia long ago. Look at the number of times he'd had to do just the same thing. The rotten jobs always came his way. Being in the police wasn't all beer and skittles, not by a long chalk. He'd always had the worst beats when he'd been in the uniformed branch, but he'd expected, when he was transferred to the C.I.D., that things would be a lot easier. And had they? Not on your life, they hadn't. The hours and hours he'd spent hanging about draughty street corners . . .

Hello, what was that? Had something moved in the shadow of the house, or had his eyes played a trick? It was surprising how easy it was to imagine you saw something . . . No, there *was* something. Somebody had flitted across the lawn into the shadow . . .

Leek pulled a pair of night glasses, which Mr. Budd had provided for his and Mackleberry's use, from his pocket and focused them on the place where the moving shadow had vanished. But there was nothing, now, to be seen. Nothing moved, only the swaying branches of the distant trees. For nearly a quarter of an hour he kept the glasses to his eyes, hopefully expectant, but there was no sign of any living thing. At last, with a sigh and aching arms, he lowered the night glasses and blinked to ease his strained eyes. There was nothing now, but he could have sworn there *had* been something. He had not imagined that quick, gliding shadow. *Somebody* had crossed the lawn and gone round to the back of the house . . .

He took out his handkerchief and wiped his wet face. There was nothing he could do except watch. The ornate iron gates of the drive were locked at night, and, although he might have found another way in, it would mean leaving his post; and if any of the Brockwell family should leave the house while he was away there would be trouble. His instructions were to follow any of the Brockwells if they went out and not to go chasing shadows . . . He kept an added vigilance, however, but an hour passed without anything happening.

When two o'clock struck from St. Peter's Church he produced the packet of sandwiches and thermos flask of coffee which he had brought to sustain him, and munched and drank, glad of something to do, although he was neither hungry nor thirsty. The hot coffee warmed him, however, and helped to stave off the sleepiness which threatened at this hour. He thought of Mr. Budd comfortably tucked up in his bed at the Peal o' Bells, and all the other people who were sleeping normally, and the contrast seemed to make his unpleasant duty all the harder . . .

Three o'clock. Only another hour and then Mackleberry would be back. It was getting colder, although the rain had ceased. He finished the last of the coffee, and stamped his feet to try and get some feeling back into them. The whole of his thin body was cold and clammy with the damp that oozed up from the ground on which he stood . . .

Four o'clock. The welcome hour tolled out and Leek gave a grunt of relief. The long night was nearly over. In a few seconds Mackleberry would arrive to take over . . .

The sergeant came, five minutes late, and Leek thankfully handed over the night glasses and hurried as quickly as he could back to Mrs. Cutts's hospitable cottage and the bed which awaited him . . .

9

Mr. Tom Custer woke to the shrill summons of the alarm clock by the head of his bed and cursed its noisy clamour long and heartily. It had wakened him in the middle of a particularly pleasant dream, in which he had found himself standing in the vaults of the Bank of England surrounded by stacks of new, crisp notes and great heaps of glittering gold bars. To find himself in the narrow bed in his small room, with the grey morning light filtering reluctantly through the chinks in the curtains, was decidedly an anti-climax.

He stopped the alarm clock, yawned, and got out of bed. Pouring some water into a basin, he washed sparingly and huddled himself into an old pair of flannel trousers and a torn pullover. This was his habitual morning attire. Later, before the family rose, he would shave and dress himself in his conventional black.

The maids were busy cleaning and

dusting when he came down the stairs, and he found the cook in the kitchen drinking a cup of tea preparatory to starting on the breakfasts. In the Brockwell family there was no laid breakfast. They each breakfasted individually in their own rooms from trays which were taken up to them.

The cook, a stout woman with a continual grievance, presented Mr. Custer with a cup of tea and remarked that it was 'an 'orrible mornin',' a statement with which he entirely agreed.

'Not that it make much difference ter *me* wot the mornin's like, or any other part o' the day, for that matter,' continued Mrs. Bleecher, 'stuck in this 'ere kitchen all the hours God give me.'

'Well, you've got two breakfasts less ter get now,' said Mr. Custer, with a grin.

'Which makes no difference at all,' declared Mrs. Bleecher, determined to accept nothing that would ease her hard lot. 'Five breakfasts or three, it makes no difference.'

'Maybe yer'll 'ave less before long,' said Mr. Custer, gulping his tea.

'Lawks o' mercy!' cried the cook. 'Whatever do yer mean? You don't expect there's goin' ter be any *more* murders, do yer?'

'You never can tell,' said Mr. Custer, cheerfully. 'I don't see why this feller, whoever 'e is, should stop at two . . . '

'Well, if there's any more, I'm packin' up,' declared Mrs. Bleecher, emphatically. 'If it wasn't that the money's good I wouldn't be 'ere now, I can tell you. For a more unpleasant lot I've never worked for, an' that's a fact. Common as dirt, they are, an' treats yer like dirt, which is a thing the real gentry never does, an' I should know, 'avin' worked for some of the best families in the land . . . '

'Like me,' said Mr. Custer. 'I've worked for Royalty, I 'ave.' He did not mention that it was sewing mailbags at Pentonville. 'They're a queer lot, ain't they?' he went on, staring into his teacup thoughtfully.

'Queer!' Mrs. Bleecher sniffed. 'I declare, Mr. Custer, I've never known such a queer lot before — no, not in all my experience. Always rowin' and quarrellin' like they are. As I said, if it weren't that the money was good I'd be off ter-morrer, an' I shall if there's any more murderin'. You never know where that sort o' thing's going to end . . . Wot is it, Phoebe?'

'Tea ready?' asked the maid, appearing at the kitchen door.

'Not fer a minute or two,' said Mrs. Bleecher. 'Can't quite work by magic, you know. Yer'll 'ave to wash yer face before yer take it up. You can't go with that smut acrost yer nose.'

Phoebe went over and examined herself in a small mirror. The offending smut was large and obvious. She picked up a corner of her apron, licked it with her tongue, and rubbed her nose vigorously.

'Gone now,' she announced, happily.

Mrs. Bleecher set three morning tea-trays with a cup and saucer, milk-jug, sugar-basin, and slop-bowl. She filled the three small jugs with milk and put tea from a large caddy into the three teapots, carried them over to the range and filled them with water from the boiling kettle.

'There you are,' she said, bringing them back to the table and setting each on its separate tray.

'I'll bet the old man'll be glad of 'is tea,'

remarked Mr. Custer, with a chuckle. 'Must've got a mouth like the bottom of a canary cage this mornin'.'

'Drinkin' again, was 'e?' asked Mrs. Bleecher.

'Swimmin' in it,' answered Mr. Custer, lighting a cigarette. 'Funny thing, it don't seem to affect 'im much . . . '

'It don't some people,' said Mrs. Bleecher, pouring herself out another cup of tea. 'It's just on eight, Phoebe. You'd best be getting along.'

The maid put the three small trays on to one big one, picked it up and departed.

'Girls in service ain't wot they used ter be,' said Mrs. Bleecher, shaking her head. 'Slovenly, that's wot they are. No pride in theirselves or their jobs . . . '

'Nuthin' ain't what it used ter be,' said Mr. Custer. 'Too many officials, that's the trouble.' He had nearly said 'policemen,' but altered it in time.

'I don't know wot a man like you's doin' in a job like this,' said Mrs. Bleecher, looking at him curiously.

Mr. Custer thought it was better not to tell her.

'Because the money's good — same as you,' he answered.

'I'd like ter know 'ow they got all their money,' said the cook, sipping the strong, over-sweet tea. 'They didn't come by it honest, I'll be bound.'

Mr. Custer inhaled a lungful of smoke, but made no reply. The origin of Henry Brockwell's wealth did not trouble him. The only thing that did was that he had evolved a perfectly good scheme for side-tracking a good portion of it into his own pocket, a scheme which had been nipped in the bud by the appearance of Mr. Budd. He smiled at the phrase. The arrival of that fat and sleepy-eyed man had been something of a shock, and he had had to hastily reconsider his plans. It looked as if he might have to abandon them altogether, for it would be much too risky to attempt anything of the sort under the nose of the man who knew him so well. It was a great pity, because he'd had everything set for the biggest clean-up of his life.

'Well,' he said, getting down from his perch on a corner of the big table and stretching, 'this won't do. I'd better . . . '

He was interrupted by a scream. It was not a loud scream, but it was distinct and clear, and it was followed by a crash of breaking china.

'That's Phoebe,' said Mrs. Bleecher. 'Wot can be the matter with the girl . . . ?'

But Mr. Custer was already out of the kitchen and she finished her remark to empty air. The reason for the faintness of the scream was because it had come from upstairs, he concluded, and he went racing up the big staircase two steps at a time. He heard doors opening as he reached the landing and saw Henry Brockwell, flushed of face and bleary-eyed, his hair awry, struggling into a dressing-gown.

'What's the matter?' he demanded, thickly. 'Who's kicking up that infernal racket?'

'I don't know, sir,' said Mr. Custer. 'I was in the kitchen . . . '

Mrs. Brockwell appeared at the door of her bedroom; her face, without its make-up, was grey and mottled.

'What's the matter — what's happened?' she called, shrilly.

'I've just asked that myself,' snapped her husband, crossly. 'Nobody seems to know . . . '

But somebody did know. Phoebe knew. She was leaning up against the door-post of a room farther along the corridor, and at her feet was a scattered collection of broken china.

'It's Mr. James,' she wailed. 'It's Mr. James . . . '

Tommy Custer sucked in his breath quickly and pushed his way past her. James Brockwell lay on his back in the bed and the sheets were still wet with the blood that had welled from his chest. His eyes were wide open and staring and there was a look of surprised terror on his unpleasant face . . .

'My God!' The hoarse whisper came from Henry Brockwell over Mr. Custer's shoulder. 'Look . . . look there . . . on the pillow by his head . . . '

Tom Custer looked and saw. A playing-card — the Queen of Diamonds.

Part Three

The Queen of Diamonds

1

Doctor Wakefield, the police surgeon, finished his examination and straightened up.

'He was killed with a long, rather thin-bladed knife,' he announced, unemotionally. 'It pierced the heart, severing one of the larger blood vessels, and was driven with considerable force. Death, which must have been almost instantaneous, took place in the region of two o'clock in the morning. That's about all I can tell you, gentlemen, until after the postmortem.'

'Thank you, doctor,' murmured Mr. Budd, and he looked at Superintendent Tidworthy. Tidworthy, an anxious and worried man, pursed his lips and scratched the side of his face. Tom Custer had rung up the police station at Bedlington with the incredible news. Tidworthy, who had just come in, collected the police surgeon, a photographer and finger-print man, drove over to Long Millford, picked up Mr.

Budd at the Peal o' Bells, and arrived at The Croft in under an hour after the discovery had been made.

'There's no sign of the weapon, so he must have taken it away with 'im,' he said.

Mr. Budd nodded.

'He took the knife an' left his card,' he said. 'The Queen o' Diamonds this time. That still leaves the King an' the Ace. I wonder when he'll play *them* . . . '

'He won't play them at all!' exploded Tidworthy, with energy. 'This can't go on. We've got to stop any more . . . '

'That's what we tried to do last time,' grunted the big man. 'An' we thought we'd fixed it, didn't we? With a watch on the 'ouse from dusk till dawn . . . '

'I wonder if Leek or Mackleberry saw anything?' interrupted Tidworthy. 'They may have done . . . '

'I've sent for Leek,' said Mr. Budd, wearily. ''E ought ter be 'ere at any moment. Accordin' ter Custer there's a winder on the ground floor with a broken pane o' glass near the catch an' muddy footprints on the floor. That's 'ow he came an' went . . . '

'We'll have the servants up, and find out if any of 'em heard or saw anything during the night,' said the superintendent.

'You won't want me any more at the moment,' interposed Wakefield, 'so I'll get along. See you later.' He nodded curtly and went out.

Tidworthy rang the bell and after a few minutes' delay Tom Custer appeared, white-faced and unshaven, and still dressed in his pullover and flannel trousers.

'Listen,' said Tidworthy, sharply. 'Where do you sleep?'

'At the top of the 'ouse,' replied Mr. Custer.

'Did you hear anything during the night?'

Mr. Custer shook his head.

'Not a blinkin' thing,' he declared. 'When I goes ter bed I'm so tired nuthin' 'ud wake me . . . '

'What a thing it is to 'ave a clear conscience,' murmured Mr. Budd. 'Who gave you that letter you brought in the other evenin', Tommy?'

Mr. Custer was taken by surprise and momentarily off his guard. A startled expression crossed his thin face, but he quickly recovered himself.

'Wot letter?' he demanded.

'You know very well what letter,' said Mr. Budd, smoothly. 'There was only *one* letter . . . '

'I told yer. I found it in the 'all,' answered Mr. Custer, and the big man slowly shook his head.

'I know you did, Tommy,' he said, gently. 'I've bin wonderin' why you was telling lies . . . '

'It was the truth,' declared Tom Custer, earnestly. 'If I never move from 'ere . . . '

'You wouldn't like ter spend the rest of yer life stuck in that one spot, I'm sure,' said Mr. Budd, with mild sarcasm. 'It 'ud be almost as bad as spendin' it in gaol, wouldn't it? So come across, Tommy. Who gave yer that letter?'

'Nobody,' said Mr. Custer, stubbornly. 'I don't know what you're talkin' about . . . '

'H'm, that's a pity,' remarked Mr. Budd, sorrowfully. 'A great pity. The cells at Bedlington ain't very comfortable. They lack all the modern conveniences of — say — Cannon Row . . . '

''Ere, wot are you gettin' at?' demanded Tom Custer, in alarm. 'Wot 'ave the cells at Bedlington got ter do with me?'

'You'll see,' said Mr. Budd, and his voice was suddenly very stern. 'You'd better take 'im, Superintendent . . . ' He winked at Tidworthy behind Custer's back.

'You can't do that ter me,' said Tom Custer, in consternation. 'You can't bring no charge against me . . . '

'Withholdin' evidence likely to be beneficial ter the p'lice,' broke in Mr. Budd, severely. 'There may be other charges later, but that'll do ter be goin' on with . . . '

'You've no proof,' said Mr. Custer, now thoroughly alarmed. 'It's a blinkin' frame-up, that's what it is . . . '

'An' you'll make a pretty picture in that frame,' said the big man. 'So let's cut out the cackle an' get goin' . . . '

''Ere, wait a jiffy,' said Tom Custer, suddenly making up his mind. 'I'll come clean.'

'Now that's what I call a sensible feller,' declared Mr. Budd, nodding his approval. 'Why didn't you do that in the first place,

Tommy? It'd 'ave saved a lot of argument.'

'I promised I wouldn't say nuthin',' said Mr. Custer, 'an' I don't like breakin' me word, see. But I s'pose it don't matter much now. It was the gal wot give me that letter — Sandra Brockwell.'

If he had said that it was the Archbishop of Canterbury, Tidworthy could not have looked more astonished.

'Sandra Brockwell?' he repeated, incredulously.

'Tha's right,' said Mr. Custer. 'She give it me.'

'But . . . ' began the bewildered superintendent.

'What did she say when she gave it to you?' interpolated Mr. Budd.

'She just said would I bring it in an' say I'd found it in the 'all,' replied Tom Custer.

'Oh, she said that, did she?' Mr. Budd pinched his fleshy nose, an operation that made him squint fearfully. 'An' *when* did she say an' do all this, eh?'

'Just afore tea-time the same day,' said Mr. Custer. 'She come to me an' she says: 'Custer, there's a detective comin' from

Scotland Yard this evenin'. While 'e's talkin' to my father bring this in an' say you found it in the 'all.' An' then she give me the letter an' a quid.'

'An' she made you promise not to say anything about it coming from her, eh?' murmured the big man.

'Tha's right,' agreed Tom Custer.

'H'm, interestin' an' peculiar,' said Mr. Budd. '*Very* interestin' an' *very* peculiar. Now I wonder . . . ?'

What he wondered was not destined to be divulged at that moment. The arrival of Leek interrupted him.

'I got 'ere as soon as I could,' said the sergeant, shambling into the room in an unusual hurry. 'I was in bed an' asleep when I got yer message. This is a pretty kettle o' fish, ain't it?'

'Plenty that's fishy, but nuthin' to do with any kettles,' said Mr. Budd. 'Now you just keep quiet fer a bit, will you? We'll 'ear what you've got ter say later on.'

The aggrieved Leek, not a little resentful at having been dragged from his bed, and then treated in this cavalier manner, retired to a corner and subsided into a chair. Mr. Budd turned his attention once more to Tom Custer.

'I s'pose this is the truth you're tellin' us?' he said. 'It wouldn't be just a story you've made up . . . '

'If I never move from 'ere . . . ' began Mr. Custer, indignantly.

'I know all about that,' interrupted Mr. Budd, impatiently. 'That don't mean a thing . . . '

'It seems funny to me,' interpolated Tidworthy, frowning. 'Why should Miss Brockwell have given you that letter?'

'How should I know why?' said Tom Custer. 'I ain't a blinkin' thought-reader. All I can tell yer is that she did.'

'Didn't she say anythin' when she give it to you?' asked Mr. Budd.

'Only wot I told you,' answered Tommy Custer. 'Blimey, I can't tell yer somethink wot didn't 'appen, can I?'

'I hope not,' said Mr. Budd. 'If you started doin' silly things like that you might find yerself in trouble.' He thought for a moment. 'All right,' he went on. 'Let's see the rest of the servants an' then we'll tackle the fam'ly . . . '

'It's no good yer seein' the old man,' said Mr. Custer, with a grimace. 'He's dead ter the world . . . '

'What do you mean? Drunk?' asked Tidworthy.

'Blind as a perishin' coot,' replied Custer, expressively. ' 'E's lying on 'is bed with a h'empty bottle o' Johnnie Walker on the floor beside 'im, breathin' like a pig with the croup! Wish I was the same,' he added. 'All this is gettin' me down . . . '

'Go and send the rest of the servants up,' ordered Mr. Budd, and Custer took his departure.

'Now,' he said, turning to Leek. 'What 'ave you got ter say?'

The sergeant had very little to say. He related what he had seen during the hours of his watch and Mr. Budd grunted.

'That must have been the murderer,' he said. 'Pity you didn't get a closer look. 'Owever, you can't be blamed for that . . . '

They questioned the servants one by one, but none of them had heard anything during the night. While the photographer and finger-print man were busy, they went down and inspected the broken window that Tom Custer had mentioned. It was in the morning-room, and one of the panes near the latch had been broken. The glass lay scattered on the polished floor and some of it had apparently been trodden on, for it was ground into the wood of the floor.

'This is how he got in,' said Tidworthy. 'Let's go outside . . . '

They went outside. Beyond the window was a smooth stone walk that would carry no traces. There were marks in plenty on a gravel path near, but they were confused and offered no prospect of a clue.

Just as they had returned to the house the Chief Constable arrived.

'This is terrible,' he said. 'Terrible. It looks, now, as if you were right, Superintendent. Somebody *is* trying to wipe out the whole family.'

'I'm afraid so, sir,' agreed Mr. Budd. His voice was a little despondent. He felt unhappily responsible for this third killing. He had foreseen its possibility, and the steps he had taken to prevent it had proved inadequate. But how could he have guessed that the murderer would take the risk of breaking in . . . ?

'Have you seen Brockwell?' asked Major Toppington. 'We ought to . . . '

'Brockwell ain't in a condition to see anybody, sir,' said Mr. Budd. ''E's drunk.'

The Chief Constable gave vent to an irritable ejaculation.

'Drunk?' he echoed. 'Good heavens — at this hour of the morning . . . '

'I rather think 'e's in a panic,' said the big man, 'or was until the drink made 'im unconscious.'

'Well, when he recovers we've got to make him talk,' said Major Toppington. 'If he knows what, or who, is at the bottom of this business he's got to tell us. This can't be allowed to go on. We can't have any more killing . . . '

'We won't, sir,' said Mr. Budd. 'I'm goin' to propose that Leek an' I stay in this 'ouse from now until this affair is over, an' make *certain* that there'll be no more.'

'You'll have to get Brockwell's permission, of course. We can't insist . . . ' He frowned. 'It's a confoundedly queer business,' he said, shaking his head. 'What's the motive? That's what we want — the motive. Was there another playing-card in this case?'

'Yes, sir,' murmured Mr. Budd. 'The Queen of Diamonds.'

'Damn it, what the devil does it mean?' growled Major Toppington. 'If it wasn't so deadly serious you'd think it was some schoolboy's joke . . . the kind of thing we used to read about in the penny bloods when we were boys . . . '

'Yes, sir,' remarked Mr. Budd. 'That's exactly what it *is* like.'

'You've heard nothing yet from the Yard?' asked Major Toppington, in the tone of voice that expects a negative.

Mr. Budd shook his head.

'No, sir. They've 'ardly had time.'

'I suppose not.' The Chief Constable twitched his shoulders impatiently. 'And we don't know whether there'll be anything when you do. I wonder if Mrs. Brockwell could help us?'

196

'I doubt it,' said Mr. Budd. 'The girl may have known somethin'.'

'Which girl? You mean Sandra?'

'Yes, sir.' The big man told him what they had learned about the letter from Tom Custer.

'H'm, that *does* look as though she knew something,' said Major Toppington, thoughtfully. 'But why on earth should she have sent that letter in the way she did? What was she hoping to gain by it?'

The big man shrugged his shoulders.

'Queer thing to do, wasn't it?' he remarked. 'Maybe she wanted to see what effect it 'ud have on her father . . . ' He yawned. 'Shall we go an' have a word with Mrs. Brockwell now? I don't think it'll lead to much, but you never can tell . . . '

2

Mrs. Brockwell was lying on a couch in her private sitting-room; a large, overcrowded apartment that looked like something from a film set. She had not dressed, or made up her face, and she looked old and raddled. Her eyes were red and swollen, there were streaks of mascara down her cheeks, and her brazen hair seemed to have lost its sheen.

She received Major Toppington, Superintendent Tidworthy, and Mr. Budd, listlessly, as though she cared very little why they were there or what they wanted.

'We are sorry to have to intrude, madam,' apologized the Chief Constable. 'But it is essential that we should ask you one or two questions . . . '

'It's all right,' she said, tonelessly. 'Ask what yer like.' She sounded weary and completely disinterested. After the usual routine questions as to whether she had heard anything during the night, when she had last seen James, what time he had gone up to bed, and what time she had gone to bed herself, Mr. Budd said:

'It seems to us, ma'am, that the most important thing about these crimes is the motive. Can you 'elp us there?'

''Ow should I?' The harsh, unlovely voice grated on their ears. 'Why don't you ask 'enry?'

'You think he knows, madam?' asked Major Toppington, quickly.

'I don't think nothink,' she retorted. 'I said, why don't yer ask 'im?'

'I'm afraid that your husband is not in a fit state to answer questions,' said the Chief Constable.

'I s'pose you mean 'e's drunk,' said Mrs. Brockwell, bluntly. 'The dirty yellow rat!'

Major Toppington winced. He was not used to such expressions on the lips of a woman. He tried to ignore the epithet, but his reaction to it was audible in his voice when he spoke again.

'Are you suggesting, madam, that your husband has reason to be afraid of someone?' he said, a little stiffly.

199

'If three of *your* family 'ad been murdered, wouldn't you be afraid?' she said. ' O' course 'e's afraid, an' so'm I, but I don't fuddle meself with drink ter bolster up my courage . . . '

'But if he's afraid — if you are afraid — you must have some reason for that fear,' persisted Major Toppington.

'Reason?' She gave an explosive laugh. 'Cor love us, ain't there reason enough? John's dead, Sandra's dead, and James's dead. 'Oo's goin' ter be the next . . . ?'

'Who do you think, ma'am?' put in Mr. Budd, very softly.

''Ow should *I* know?' she snapped. 'Maybe me . . . '

'What makes you think you should be in danger?' asked the Chief Constable.

'I didn't say I thought so,' she answered. 'I said 'maybe.' Look 'ere, mister. I don't know nuthin', so it's no good you badgerin' me. P'raps 'Enry knows somethin', p'raps 'e don't. Wait till he gets 'is senses back an' ask 'im.'

'It has occurred to us that both you and your husband may be in danger of an attack by this unknown killer,' said Major

200

Toppington. 'We think, therefore, that very stringent precautions should be taken to protect you. We suggest that Superintendent Budd and Sergeant Leek should take up a temporary residence in this house, which would enable them to keep you both under surveillance. Have you any objection to such an arrangement?'

For a moment the listlessness vanished. Mrs. Brockwell looked up alertly, and her dull eyes sparkled.

'I'm all for it,' she said. 'When can they come?'

'At once, ma'am,' said Mr. Budd. 'We'll collect our things an' bring 'em round this afternoon . . . '

'I'll tell Custer. There's plenty of room,' she said.

'Will Mr. Brockwell approve . . . ?' began the Chief Constable, but she silenced him with a quick gesture.

''im!' she said, contemptuously. 'Who cares what 'e says? 'e'll do as *I* say. You go an' fetch yer things as soon as yer like. Now you can all clear out. I'm goin' ter get dressed . . . '

'Did you notice the change in 'er?' remarked Mr. Budd, as they walked downstairs. 'She was relieved when she 'eard that we was comin'. Now *that's* very significant.'

'You mean that before she was *resigned*?' said Major Toppington.

'Yes, sir,' agreed the big man. 'That's just what she was — resigned to 'er fate. An' now she sees a possibility of escapin' it. I wonder if Brockwell 'll feel the same when 'e hears what's been arranged?'

'I should think so,' said Tidworthy. 'I should think he'd be as pleased as she was . . .'

'They're such a queer collection, it's impossible to say what they'll do, or say,' grunted the Chief Constable. 'Did you notice that there was no sign of grief? She's lost two sons and a daughter and you'd think there'd be some sort of natural grief, wouldn't you?'

Mr. Budd nodded. The point had struck him.

They met Mr. Custer in the hall. He had exchanged his old pullover and flannel trousers for the more correct garb of his calling. He heard the news that Mr. Budd and Leek were coming to stay without any marked enthusiasm.

'You expects me ter wait on yer, I s'pose?' he said. 'Cor blimey! Ain't I got enough in me packet already? Never thought I'd come down to takin' mornin' tea ter a couple of 'busies.' Just shows yer, don't it?'

'An' you'll have to mind yer Ps an' Qs, Tommy,' said Mr. Budd, warningly. 'I still can't quite get the hang of you. What you're *really* doin' here, I mean . . . '

'I told yer,' said Mr. Custer, quickly. 'I'm earnin' me livin'. Crime' — he snapped his fingers — 'crime don't pay. It's a mug's game. H'nesty is the best policy . . . '

'You've got it all off pat, ain't you?' said Mr. Budd, admiringly. 'Well, we'll be seein' you.'

Superintendent Tidworthy was saddled with the routine work of seeing the Coroner and arranging for the inquest, and Mr. Budd went back to the Peal o' Bells to pack his things and pay his bill, leaving Leek at Mrs. Cutts's cottage to do the same. The big man did not immediately attend to this, however. He wanted a quiet think and, true to his usual habit, he made himself comfortable on his bed with a cigar between his lips. Staring at the dingy ceiling through the rank blue smoke, he began to collect and marshall his thoughts into an orderly sequence. And he quickly found that it was by no means easy. There were so many gaps that he was unable to fill. The motive — that was the predominant thing. For what conceivable reason had these three people been killed? Gain? Well, who gained by their deaths? So far as was known, nobody; but it would be just as well to inquire more closely into this. He made a mental note to do this. Vengeance? What had they done to somebody to engender such a hatred? There was nothing to even hint what it could be. Perhaps there might be something in the reports from the Yard when they came. That left jealousy, and this seemed to be so unlikely that he dismissed it at once.

He wasn't getting very far, he thought irritably. Merely working round and round in the old circle. The only real facts that he possessed were three dead people and three playing-cards. Everything else was nebulous and hazy. Harriet Lake, Roger Naylor, Charles Antrim, were they important or not? And what lay behind Sandra Brockwell's extraordinary action in getting Custer to deliver that letter? It looked very much as if she had known something, but what had been her object in having the letter delivered at that particular time? Why, if she had known anything, hadn't she come out with it to the police?

A tap on the door interrupted his unprofitable musings and the muffled voice of Mr. Duffy called to him:

'There's a gentleman in the bar would like to see you, sir.'

'All right, I'll come down.' Mr. Budd swung himself reluctantly off the bed, brushed himself down, and descended to the bar.

Joshua Craven was gloomily contemplating a double whisky.

'Good evening,' he greeted. 'What will you drink?'

Mr. Budd suggested a pint of beer.

'What do *you* want?' he inquired, rather rudely.

'Heard about this latest crime and thought I'd drop in and have a little talk,' said Mr. Craven. 'Dear me, the Brockwell family seems to be rapidly diminishing, does it not? There won't be any left soon, will there?'

'Why should you think that?' demanded Mr. Budd, taking a large gulp from his tankard.

'Don't *you* think that?' asked the reporter, and without waiting for a reply: 'I hear that you're going to The Croft to stay. That was a wise move, I think. Not that I imagine it will do much good . . . '

''ow did you know?' said the big man, and Mr. Craven gave a faint smile.

'I get to hear things,' he said, evasively. 'So you did meet Roger Naylor? I said you probably would. You should take an interest in that young man. His family history would, I'm sure, prove most entertaining . . . '

'S'pose,' said Mr. Budd, 'that you stop talkin' in parables and tell me just what you're gettin' at?'

'I'm not getting at anything.' Mr. Craven drank half his whisky and stared a little sadly at the remainder. 'I'm only offering a little advice . . . '

'Why should I be interested in Naylor or his family 'istory?' said Mr. Budd.

'Because there are certain moments in it when it comes in close contact with the Brockwells,' replied Joshua Craven. 'Very close contact, indeed.'

'You seem to know quite a lot,' said Mr. Budd. ''ow did you get hold of all this information?'

'It's my business to get hold of information,' said the reporter. '*All* information becomes useful sooner or later, and when I hear things I remember them. Then something happens and I find that some scraps of information which I had previously acquired have a bearing on that happening. They illuminate it; supply a reason for something that seemed to be without reason, and the whole thing emerges. You see?'

Mr. Budd saw. This was, in fact, a brief digest of Mr. Craven's method. Everything that came his way was grist, sooner or later, for his mill.

'So you know somethin' about Naylor

that links up with the Brockwell business, an' which you knew about before there was any Brockwell business,' he remarked. 'Is that what you're tryin' to tell me?'

Joshua Craven nodded.

'Yes, that is correct,' he said. 'Roger Naylor's father died in a Canadian prison.' He drank the rest of his whisky. 'And it was Brockwell who put him there.'

3

Mr. Budd turned in at the gate of a small, semi-detached house in a quiet road in Bedlington, walked up the tiled path to the front door, and rang the bell. After an interval an elderly woman, neatly dressed in black, opened the door and looked at him inquiringly.

'Does Mr. Naylor live 'ere?' asked the big man.

The woman nodded.

'Yes, but I don't think he's in,' she said. 'I saw him go out a few minutes ago.'

Mr. Budd frowned. He hoped that it wasn't going to prove a wasted journey. He had gone to a lot of trouble to find out Naylor's address.

'D'you think e'll be long, ma'am?' he inquired.

'I really couldn't say,' she answered.

He fiddled with the lobe of his right ear.

'Maybe I could go in an' wait?' he

suggested. 'It's rather important that I should see him . . . '

The woman, whom he gathered was the landlady, received the suggestion coldly.

'I don't know that Mr. Naylor would like that,' she said, primly. 'Couldn't you call back?'

Mr. Budd said he 'supposed he could' and was turning rather reluctantly away when the woman said, looking beyond him: 'Here comes Mr. Naylor now.'

Mr. Budd looked round and saw the huge figure of Roger Naylor crossing the road. He came in the gate and stopped in surprise as he saw the big man. A look of recognition flashed in his eyes and he said, rather weakly: 'Hello.'

'Good afternoon, Mr. Naylor,' said Mr. Budd, blandly. 'I was afraid I'd missed you . . . '

'I went out to get some cigarettes,' replied Naylor. 'Did you want to see me?'

Mr. Budd nodded.

'I'd like to have a little talk with you, if you can spare the time,' he said, politely.

Naylor hesitated. The stout superintendent thought he was going to make an excuse, and then he changed his mind.

'Come in,' he said, briefly.

The elderly woman had vanished at his appearance, and he led the way to a room on the ground floor which was comfortably untidy and evidently his sitting-room.

'Sit down,' he said. 'Would you like a drink?'

'No, thank you, sir,' said Mr. Budd. He sat down in a deep armchair.

'Well, what can I do for you?' said Naylor. He was uneasy and nervous.

'I'm given to understand,' said Mr. Budd, coming straight to the point of his visit, 'that your father was acquainted with Henry Brockwell, some years ago. Is that right?'

A thin flush of red spread slowly over Roger Naylor's face. The big hands, which he had thrust into the pockets of his tweed jacket, clenched themselves.

'Who told you that?' he muttered, huskily.

'I don't think that matters very much,' murmured Mr. Budd. 'The question is, is it true?'

There was a pause before Naylor

answered. He appeared to be making up his mind.

'Yes,' he said, at last, 'yes, it's true . . . '

'The circumstances in which they knew each other wasn't very pleasant, was they?' said Mr. Budd.

'No,' said Naylor. 'No, they were not very pleasant.'

'Would you mind tellin' me all about it?' said Mr. Budd, persuasively. 'I may as well tell you that you don't *have* to if you'd rather not, but I'd be much obliged if you would . . . '

Naylor took out a packet of Players, opened it, selected a cigarette, stuck it between his lips, and lit it with a pocket lighter.

'Why,' he said, exhaling a lungful of smoke, 'do you want to know?'

'Come, come, Mr. Naylor,' said Mr. Budd, reproachfully, 'you don't 'ave ter ask that, do you? There've been three murders committed . . . '

'Three?' said Naylor, sharply. 'You mean two . . . '

'I mean three,' said Mr. Budd. 'James Brockwell was murdered in 'is bed durin'

212

the early hours of this mornin'.'

The cigarette fell from Naylor's fingers and, clumsily, he stooped and picked it up.

'I . . . I had no idea,' he stammered.

'So you see,' went on Mr. Budd, 'it's most important that we should foller up anythin' known about Brockwell's past 'istory, or anyone connected with 'im . . . '

'My father's relations with him can have nothing to do with the murders,' said Naylor, quickly. 'My father has been dead for over twelve years . . . '

''e died in a prison in Canada, didn't he?' murmured Mr. Budd.

'So you know that?' said Naylor. 'There doesn't seem to be much that I *can* tell you . . . '

'There's quite a lot you can tell me,' said the big man. 'You can tell me 'ow he came to get in prison, an' what 'Enry Brockwell 'ad ter do with it.'

Naylor stared at the end of his cigarette and then looked up.

'My father went to prison in Brockwell's place,' he said. 'Brockwell 'framed' him . . . '

' 'ow?' said Mr. Budd.

'Since I suppose you will find out in any case, I may as well tell you,' said Naylor, after a few moments' consideration. He went over and shut the door. 'I was only fourteen at the time, but I was old enough to understand . . . ' He walked over to the window, stared out into the street for a minute, came back and sat down abruptly, opposite Mr. Budd. 'I'm trying to think where to start,' he said, frowning.

'Suppose you try the beginning?' suggested Mr. Budd, helpfully.

'That's the trouble — what *is* the beginning?' Naylor made a quick gesture. 'I don't know . . . ' He flung his cigarette into the fireplace and immediately lit another. 'I don't know how my father came to know Brockwell,' he continued, speaking in short, rapid sentences with long pauses in between. 'I think it must have been in a club in Montreal . . . My father was a great gambler and he would play cards with anybody . . . '

'Poker?' interjected Mr. Budd, quickly, and the other nodded.

'Yes,' he said. 'Poker was his favourite game, but he'd play anything . . . He'd spend most nights playing cards . . . Mother didn't like it, and she didn't like Brockwell. She always said that if father got mixed up with Brockwell it would lead to trouble, but he only laughed at her. He said he knew Brockwell's type well enough and he could take care of himself, but he couldn't . . . He only realized it when it was too late.'

Naylor got up and began pacing the room with long, nervous strides. 'He'd been losing money steadily over a period of weeks, and Brockwell had been raking it in . . . They played for high stakes, and his losses ran into thousands . . . One night he lost practically all he had left — a little over five thousand pounds. Brockwell had an unbeatable hand — a royal flush in diamonds — and my father got up from the table a ruined man . . . I remember my mother crying bitterly when he told her . . . It was the day after this that my father discovered that Brockwell had won by cheating . . . I don't know how he found it out, but he did, and he tackled Brockwell with it and threatened to expose him. Brockwell blustered, finally admitted it, and begged him to keep quiet, offered to refund the money and gave my father a cheque . . . Three days later my father was arrested. Brockwell had sworn the cheque he gave him was originally for only five pounds and that my father had altered it to five thousand. The bank specialist proved at the trial that the amount *had* been altered. The ink had been erased with chemicals and the larger amount written in. My father was sentenced to five years and died in prison after serving eighteen months. My mother, who never recovered from the shock of the disgrace, died a year after . . . That's the story. Not a very pretty one, is it?'

No, not a pretty one at all, thought Mr. Budd. I wonder if you realize just what this means as far as you're concerned? It gives you a strong motive for three murders and supplies an explanation for the playing-cards . . . Aloud he said:

'I s'pose Brockwell faked the cheque before he gave it to your father?'

Naylor nodded.

'That's what the defence tried to prove,' he said, 'but the prosecution laughed the suggestion to scorn . . . ' He lit another cigarette from the half-smoked butt of the other, and Mr. Budd stroked his nose.

' 've you seen Brockwell since he came to live at Long Millford?' he asked.

'No,' answered Naylor, shortly.

'Who came 'ere first?' inquired the big man, and he was surprised when Naylor answered:

'I did. I've lived here for nearly seven years.'

'What made you come to live here?'

'Well,' said Naylor, 'I've an estate business in Bedlington. Normally I should be at the office, but I wasn't feeling very well and I took the day off.'

'Is this business under your name?' asked Mr. Budd.

'Yes. Why?'

'I just wondered.' Mr. Budd transferred his hand from his nose to his right ear and gently massaged that.

'The other afternoon — when I met

you at Miss Lake's,' he said, 'was she expectin' you?'

Naylor looked surprised.

'No,' he answered. 'Why?'

Mr. Budd made no reply. He was thinking of that extra cup which Harriet Lake had set so opportunely on the tray. She had been expecting *somebody* . . .

'You've known Miss Lake a long time?' he said.

'All my life,' replied Naylor. 'She's my cousin. Her father was my mother's brother.'

4

Mr. Budd went back to Long Millford with plenty to think about. Here in the district were two people who both had the best possible reasons for hating the Brockwells. Brockwell had been the cause of bringing disgrace and death to Naylor's father, and was also the cause of Edward Lake's suicide. Indirectly he was also the cause of Naylor's mother's death. Here was a strong and plausible motive for the murders and a complete explanation for the playing-cards. It all fitted perfectly, and Naylor had just the right physique to have been able to use the pitchfork. He could produce no satisfactory alibi for any of the times when the murders had been committed, because he had, or so he said, been in bed and asleep on all three occasions. The proper thing to do would be to get a warrant issued and arrest him, but Mr. Budd hesitated. The evidence against him was strong, but there was something that worried the big man and made him uncertain.

Would Naylor, if he had decided to kill off the Brockwell family in revenge for what Henry Brockwell had done to *his* family, have left such a damning pointer as the playing-cards? Nobody but a fool would have done such a stupid thing, and Naylor, shy and nervous as he might be, was no fool. And wouldn't he also, at least, have tried to trump up some sort of an alibi for the times of the murders? Once the story of his father's relations with Brockwell came out — and it was, as he must have known, bound to come out sooner or later during the investigation — the leaving of those playing-cards was almost as good as signing his name. It was true that the average murderer did stupid things, but surely not quite as silly as this? And then, again, Naylor had been fourteen when Brockwell had framed his father over the cheque. Would he have nursed such a hatred for all those years? It was unusual and, from what Mr. Budd had seen of him, out of character. There was the possibility that his hatred of

Brockwell had been inflamed by the suicide of his uncle, Edward Lake, but surely not enough to lead to this saturnalia of murder.

And that, he suddenly thought, was a very queer thing indeed. Edward Lake must have *known* that it was Brockwell who had framed his brother-in-law. Why had he allowed himself to be swindled by a man whom he would have been suspicious of from the start? That was very strange. In fact it was ridiculous. No man, unless he was mentally deficient, would have done such a thing. But according to Harriet Lake this was exactly what her father *had* done. And would Brockwell have attempted such a trick on a member of the family he had already injured? Well, in his case, perhaps, he didn't know. The name was different and he may not have connected Lake with Naylor. But Lake couldn't have failed to have known who *he* was . . . It was all very queer . . .

Mr. Budd was still pondering on its queerness when he reached Long Millford and discovered that Leek, with the aid of the potman at the Peal o' Bells, had carted his things along to The Croft. The lean sergeant met him in the hall and his lugubrious face was, for once, slightly less despondent.

'They've done us proud,' he said. 'Feather beds an' everythin', 'ot an' cold runnin' water . . . Yer couldn't wish for anythin' more comfortable.'

'All you ever think about is yer comfort,' said Mr. Budd, reprovingly. 'A sybarite — that's what you are . . .'

'I ain't. I'm a Methodist,' corrected Leek. 'The same as me father was before me . . .'

'I don't believe you ever 'ad a father,' snarled Mr. Budd. 'Where am I?'

'You're in the room next ter me,' answered the sergeant. 'I'll take yer to it.' He led the way up the stairs. Their two rooms were on the second landing and Mr. Budd had to admit that they were very comfortable, if a little unpleasing to the eye.

'Makes yer feel like a film star,' he grunted. 'All this silk an' satin an' mirrors . . . Oh, well. P'raps we shan't be 'ere long . . .'

'Why, are you on ter somethin'?' demanded Leek.

'Quite a lot,' said Mr. Budd. 'But whether it's the right somethin' is another matter. 'ave you seen anythin' of Brockwell?'

Leek shook his thin head.

'No,' he replied. ' 'e's still sleepin' it off, I expect . . . '

'I want to 'ave a little talk with that feller,' said Mr. Budd, taking off his jacket and rolling up his shirt sleeves. 'Maybe 'e'll recover sufficiently ter put in an appearance this evenin'.'

'I ain't seen nuthin' of Mrs. Brockwell, neither,' said Leek. 'She 'ad 'er tea taken up to 'er room . . . '

'Speakin' o' tea,' broke in Mr. Budd, turning on the taps over the pink marble and chromium basin, 'what about us?'

'I've 'ad mine,' said Leek, with great satisfaction. 'That feller Custer fixed it for me. Three different sorts o' sandwiches an' all kinds o' cake . . . '

'Well, you go an' tell 'im to fix some for me,' said Mr. Budd, washing his hands vigorously, 'an' while I have it we'd better have a talk.'

The sergeant departed and the big man continued his ablutions. He washed his face, towelled himself energetically, and brushed his thinning hair. As he was resuming his jacket, Leek came back.

'Custer's bringin' you yer tea up 'ere,' he said.

Mr. Budd settled himself in an armchair and yawned.

'Sit down,' he ordered. 'You look untidy standin' about.'

With a sigh Leek folded his long form on to a chair.

'That's better,' said his superior. 'Now just you listen ter me . . . '

With great deliberation he began a recital of his interview with Roger Naylor.

'Don't seem much doubt ter me,' commented Leek, when he had finished. 'Naylor's the feller. Everythin' points to it . . . '

'That's the trouble,' murmured Mr. Budd, staring at the ceiling.

''Ow d'yer mean?' began the sergeant.

'Too much points to it,' said the big man, shaking his head. 'It's too good to be true . . . '

'I don't know what you mean,' said the puzzled Leek. ''Ere's a feller with the motive an' opportunity an' everythin'. What d'you mean by 'it bein' too good to be true'?'

'Just what I say.' Mr. Budd pursed his lips and shook his head. 'It's too much like 'avin' it put on a plate an' handed to yer . . .'

'Do you mean you don't think this feller Naylor's got anythin' ter do with it?' demanded the astonished Leek.

'Oh, yes, I think 'e's got everythin' ter do with it,' answered Mr. Budd. 'But I just don't think he's the murderer . . .'

Before Leek could comment on this surprising statement there was a tap on the door and Mr. Custer entered with a laden tray.

'Never thought I'd come down so low as waitin' on a lot o' perishin' p'licemen,' he said, disgustedly, putting the tray down on a small table. 'Blimey! What a lark.'

'You can think yerself lucky you're able to, me lad,' said Mr. Budd, severely. 'You might be where policemen 'ud be waitin' on you.'

Mr. Custer regarded him with a resentful eye.

'Is that another threat?' he demanded. 'Cor blimey! Why don't you pop me in the cooler an' 'ave done with it?'

'Because you're much too useful where you are,' said Mr. Budd, munching a sandwich. 'Where I can keep an eye on you . . .'

'Wotcher mean?' said Tommy Custer, suspiciously.

'Just that I'm very curious to know what you're doin' here,' said the big man, thickly, his mouth full of watercress sandwich. 'You know, Tommy, I never believed that story of yours about honest work. You couldn't run straight if you tried for a 'undred years. You come 'ere to work some kind o' graft an' I want to know what it is.'

Into Mr. Custer's face came a look of outraged virtue.

'Disbelievin' bleeder, ain't yer?' he said. 'Cor strike me pink, you wouldn't believe yer own mother, would yer?'

'Not if she told me you'd given up bein' crooked,' agreed Mr. Budd, complacently. He poured himself out a cup of tea carefully. 'Between you an' me, what *did* you come 'ere for?'

'After what I told yer, I consider that an h'insult,' said Mr. Custer, and he stalked from the room with great dignity.

Mr. Budd laughed until his great stomach shook like a jelly.

''e's a funny feller, Tommy,' he remarked. 'Quite a character.' He helped himself to a cake. 'Well, now,' he went on, 'let's get to business . . . We've got ter fix up about ter-night. You'd better get to bed early an' get up about two an' come an' relieve me. I'll keep watch until then . . . '

Leek's expression was not very enthusiastic.

'Where are we keepin' watch?' he asked.

Mr. Budd considered.

'The best place'll be in the corridor outside their rooms,' he answered. 'We'll make sure that the windows are fastened and that nobody can get in *that* way. I think that should put a stop to the killer's little plan.'

But it didn't. There was to be a fourth murder, and it happened in circumstances that Mr. Budd candidly admitted were completely impossible.

5

Four days passed slowly without anything eventful happening, and Mr. Budd began to find life at The Croft a little boring. After a great deal of consideration, the big man had decided to take no steps as yet regarding Roger Naylor, beyond having him closely watched. In this he had the full agreement of Major Toppington, to whom he had confided the result of his visit to Bedlington. The Chief Constable's opinion coincided with his own that to arrest Naylor, until they had more evidence, would be a bad move. An unobtrusive man, however, made his appearance in the road in which Naylor lived and discreetly followed him wherever he went, his place being taken at stated intervals by another as unobtrusive as himself. There had as yet been no word from the Yard, but Mr. Budd had tackled Henry Brockwell concerning Naylor's story. That unpleasant man made no effort to deny it, although he stoutly affirmed that it was not he who had altered the cheque, but George Naylor. There had been no question of cheating at cards, either. Naylor had invented that to bolster up his story of the alleged frame-up. He had given him a cheque for five pounds in payment of a card debt — it was the balance of a larger sum which he had paid in cash — and Naylor had altered it with chemicals and made it for five thousand. And Brockwell stuck to this story. Nothing would shift him. He also declared that he had no knowledge that Lake had been a relation of the Naylors. That transaction had been unlucky, that was all. There was no question of any swindle. He, himself, had lost money. It was just sheer bad luck. Lake could just as easily have made money instead of losing it. People shouldn't speculate unless they could afford it and were prepared to lose.

He had no idea that Naylor's son was living at Bedlington. He knew that Harriet Lake was living there, but not Naylor. Mr. Budd got the impression that he was scared at hearing of the proximity of Roger Naylor and, although he professed to pooh-pooh the suggestion that he was responsible for the murders, that he wasn't nearly so sure *inside* as he tried to make out outwardly. The big man thought that he was most likely speaking the truth when he said he had not known that Naylor was living in the district. If he had, and thought that he had any cause to fear him, he would hardly have built the house at Long Millford. And that was a question that Mr. Budd felt still had to be answered. Why *had* he come to live at Long Millford?

As the time went by and he seemed to be making little headway, the fat superintendent began to grow irritable and restless. Life within The Croft was monotonous and got on his nerves. There were constant quarrels and bickerings between Brockwell and his wife and they seemed to live in a state of mutual dislike that occasionally blazed out into open hatred. The watch was kept religiously. Sergeant Mackleberry and another man took it in turns to patrol the outside of the house, and either Leek or Mr. Budd were on duty in the corridor outside the Brockwells' bedroom doors as soon as they had retired for the night.

Nobody could reach them from outside, and nobody could reach them from within. They were, once dusk had fallen, as closely guarded as prisoners in a cell. Mr. Budd was taking no chances again. He had not forgotten what the Coroner had said at the inquest on James Brockwell, and it rankled.

He had said, at the conclusion of his short address to the jury: 'This is the third murder to be perpetrated in this district within a period of six weeks, and the murderer is still at large. I cannot help thinking that there must be something radically wrong with the methods adopted by the police for such a state of things to exist. This last crime was committed under the very noses of the Scotland Yard detectives who had been called in to assist the local police in their investigations . . . '

There was more of it on the same lines, and the newspapers had not been backward in following the Coroner's lead.

They issued a concerted protest against the inability of Scotland Yard to have protected the last two victims of the unknown murderer. This howl of dissatisfaction resulted in several questions in the House of Commons, which, in turn, resulted in a terse note from the Home Office to the Chief Commissioner. This was passed on, with a caustic comment, to Colonel Blair, who immediately — and by no means politely — demanded a full explanation from Mr. Budd. The explanation only produced a slightly mollifying effect. The Assistant Commissioner made it crystal-clear that unless there were satisfactory results in the very near future, Mr. Budd would be taken off the case and someone else, more competent to deal with it, put in his place.

In consequence of all this, and because he felt that to a certain extent it was justified, the stout superintendent was bad-tempered and depressed. His record was exceptionally good and he had no desire to spoil it by the humiliating experience of being recalled to the Yard. It was to his credit that in these trying circumstances he made no attempt to offer a sop to his superiors, and the public, by arresting Naylor. He firmly believed that it would be a false move and refused to be tempted. There was, he felt, a great deal more behind the 'playing-card murders' — as the newspapers called it — that as yet had not been glimpsed, but of which he was hazily conscious; a dark and horrible something that was the result of a carefully conceived plan . . .

The fifth day since he and Leek had come to live at The Croft dawned inauspiciously, giving no hint of what lay in wait along the track of time. It was a wet day, with a steady downfall of rain from a sky the colour of lead. It went on raining all the morning and throughout the afternoon, until everything outside was sodden and dripping, and inside, dull and depressing. Mr. Budd wandered about the house disconsolately, meeting nobody but the servants, for Henry Brockwell had gone back to his room immediately after breakfast and Mrs. Brockwell had not put in an appearance at all. Just after tea the rain stopped and the big man decided, much as he loathed exercise, to go for a short walk and get some air. Leaving Leek to look after things, he put on a raincoat and walked down to the village. It was very close and clammy, but the smell of the wet earth, mingled with the perfume of the hawthorn and the lilac, was refreshing, and by the time he reached the narrow High Street he felt better. The oppression which had weighed heavily on him all day lifted and he began to feel more normal.

As he was passing Doctor Middlesham's house, the door opened and Middlesham and Clarissa came out. The doctor hailed him and he stopped.

'Hello,' he said. 'I hear you've left the Peal o' Bells and gone to act as personal bodyguard to Brockwell and his wife?'

'That's right,' said Mr. Budd.

'How do you like it?' asked Middlesham.

'I don't like it at all, sir,' admitted Mr. Budd, candidly. 'But it's one o' those things that 'as to be done. We can't have any more murders . . .'

'You know what I think?' said Middlesham. 'I think that there's a lunatic at large. Oh,

I don't mean an obvious lunatic. I mean somebody who looks as sane and normal as you or I, but is cursed with a homicidal kink . . . '

'Only directed against the Brockwells, sir?' said Mr. Budd, doubtfully.

'Yes, why not?' demanded Middlesham. 'These things take queer turns. I had a patient once who used to go into fits of hysterical rage at the sight of rhubarb and custard. In every other respect he was perfectly normal . . . '

Clarissa laughed.

'I don't believe *that*,' she said.

'It's an absolute fact,' declared Middlesham.

'I don't think we've got a lunatic ter deal with here, sir,' said Mr. Budd, shaking his head. 'These killings were planned and carried out by somebody who's remarkably clever . . . '

'Homicidal maniacs are pretty cunning as a rule,' said Middlesham.

'But not in *this* way,' Mr. Budd disagreed. 'There's something more at the back of it than that.'

'Have you any reason for saying that?'

said Clarissa. 'Or is it just an opinion?'

'Well, miss,' replied Mr. Budd, non-committally. 'Maybe it's just a little more than an opinion . . . '

'I thought you'd got something up your sleeve,' said Middlesham. 'It's no good asking what it is, I suppose?'

'I don't think I could tell you if I wanted to,' remarked the big man, slowly. 'It's one o' them things that you can't put into words very easily . . . '

'Uh, huh,' broke in the girl, warningly. 'Look who's coming.'

Mr. Budd followed the direction of her eyes and saw Mr. Joshua Craven approaching on the other side of the street.

'Do you know 'im, miss?' he asked, and she nodded.

'Yes, he's been pestering Father and me with questions,' she answered.

'What, again?' said Middlesham, frowning.

'Yes. The man's becoming a nuisance,' she said. 'He's always hanging about the house and waylaying you when you come out . . . '

'Tell him if he doesn't stop annoying

you, you'll send for the police,' said Middlesham. 'That ought to scare him.'

'It 'ud take more than that ter scare Joshua Craven,' murmured Mr. Budd, watching the approaching figure of the reporter. He wondered if Mr. Craven would cross over and speak to them, but he didn't. He only raised his hat and passed by on the other side.

'A dangerous man,' said Mr. Budd, shaking his head. 'A *very* dangerous man. You should never tell him anything, miss, that you don't want to become public property . . .'

'I haven't any very dreadful secrets,' she said, laughing.

'They don't have to be dreadful,' said Mr. Budd, seriously. 'That feller once spent three weeks getting friendly with the Duchess of Bulfroy's footman, an' all he wanted ter know was whether 'er grace liked Gruyère cheese . . . It's a fact,' he added, quickly, as Doctor Middlesham chuckled. 'An' d'you know what it led to?'

'No, what?' asked the girl, curiously.

'It led to the institution of divorce proceedings by the duke,' said Mr. Budd, gravely. 'Craven wrote an article, an' although he didn't mention no names, everybody knew who 'e was writin' about. So you see, you can't be too careful . . .'

'But I don't like Gruyère cheese,' said Clarissa, smiling.

'No more did the duchess,' replied Mr. Budd, 'an' that was the trouble. You can't be too careful when you're dealin' with a feller like Craven.'

'How did it lead to a divorce?' asked Clarissa. 'The cheese, I mean . . .'

'Well, it' ud take a long time ter tell,' said Mr. Budd, 'an' I've got to be gettin' back ter The Croft, but there was a feller what *did* like Gruyère cheese, an' 'e was a friend o' the duke's. There was also a little shop in Soho what sold a particular brand that this feller liked, an' the duchess was a reg'lar customer fer it . . . Yer see 'ow little things lead ter bigger things?'

Clarissa was staring into vacancy, and all the amusement had left her face.

'Yes,' she said. 'Yes, I see.'

'Well, I must be gettin' along,' said Mr. Budd. 'My advice to you is — keep very clear o' Joshua Craven.'

He continued his walk, and his big face was thoughtful.

What did Craven hope to get out of Clarissa Pipp-Partington and her father? Something important or he wouldn't be wasting his time — Mr. Craven never wasted that precious commodity. And what was it that the girl had suddenly remembered she had told him, that she would much rather she had not?

He found himself back at The Croft without an answer to either of these questions.

6

That long-remembered evening, which was to present Mr. Budd with the most difficult problem of his life, began quietly enough. It was the big man's turn for early duty, which meant that he would be on guard inside the house until 2 a.m.; and Leek went to bed as soon as he returned, to prepare himself for the watch from two until the dawn. Sergeant Mackleberry was already at his post outside the house, and would remain there until he was relieved at two o'clock. It was his job to patrol the grounds in the immediate vicinity of the house, making a complete circle every twenty minutes, and it would be a clever person indeed who would be able to escape his vigilance.

Mr. Budd went straight up to his room when he came in, washed and tidied himself up, and then came down to the drawing-room. It was empty. He helped himself to a modest Johnnie Walker with a lot of soda and drank it slowly. He would have preferred beer, but beer was not easily obtainable in Mr. Brockwell's house. When he had finished his drink he wandered out into the hall, but there was nobody about. He might have been alone in the place, so still and silent was it. The previous night he had had dinner alone in the great dining-room that was so like an hotel, without the life and bustle, and he wondered if this would happen again to-night. Apparently not, for when he looked in he saw that three places had been laid at one end of the long table at which thirty people could have sat with ease.

He felt restless and ill at ease and, remembering that sensation afterwards, wondered if some queer premonition had come to him. At the time, however, he merely thought that he was a little out of sorts. He went back to the drawing-room and was staring moodily out of the window at the dull greyness of the evening when Brockwell came in. He greeted Mr. Budd with a surly grunt and went straight over to the whisky decanter.

Pouring out nearly half a tumbler of whisky, he drank it neat, wiped his lips on the back of his hand, and glowered at Mr. Budd.

''ow long are you an' that sergeant feller goin' to stop 'ere?' he demanded, harshly.

'Until the danger's over,' replied Mr. Budd.

'When's that goin' ter be?'

'When we've caught the murderer.'

Brockwell gave a short, rasping laugh.

'Looks as though you'll be 'ere for ever at the rate you're goin',' he said, unpleasantly. 'I'm gettin' pretty tired o' havin' my house full of policemen . . . '

'Maybe you'd rather be found dead with a playin' card beside you?' suggested Mr. Budd, not without malice.

'Now, look 'ere, my good man . . . ' began Brockwell, angrily, but Mr. Budd cut him short.

'*You* look 'ere,' he snapped. 'I don't want ter stay in this house a second longer'n what I can 'elp. I don't like bein' 'ere any more'n what you like my bein' 'ere. But I've got my job ter do, an' this is the way it's got ter be done. So we've both got to make the best of it.'

Brockwell's reddish face flushed to a deeper hue. Mr. Budd expected an outburst, but it didn't come. Instead there was a short silence, and then Brockwell said in the mildest possible manner: 'Sorry. Didn't mean ter be rude. I guess my nerves are bad what with one thing an' another. Have a drink?'

Mr. Budd declined the invitation, and Brockwell shrugged his shoulders and poured out another for himself. He was, thought Mr. Budd, strung up to a tension that was very near breaking-point, and he concluded that the man was really half-crazed with fear. All this boorish bombast was a kind of defensive cloak.

Mrs. Brockwell came in. Mr. Budd bowed politely and she acknowledged it with a fairly gracious 'good evening.' She was heavily made up and had taken the trouble to dress herself with elaborate care. The result was like a rather shoddy chorus girl from a cheap touring revue, although the dress was an expensive model. She ignored her husband completely, and the look he gave her was full of hatred.

'What 'ave you got yerself up like a dog's dinner for?' he demanded, rudely. 'Who d'you think you're goin' ter vamp . . . ?'

'You shut up!' she snapped. 'What's it got ter do with you 'ow I dress? It ain't *your* money . . . '

'You look like something off a Christmas tree,' he snapped. 'Or a bit of old mutton tryin' to look like lamb . . . '

'That's better than lookin' an' behavin' like a pig!' she said, angrily. 'I s'pose you've bin drinkin' again . . . ?'

'I'll drink as much as I like,' he growled.

'You can drink yerself to death for all I care!' she retorted, 'an' good riddance . . . '

Brockwell opened his mouth to reply, but whatever stream of abuse he had planned was stopped before he could give it utterance by the booming of the dinner gong. Instead, he gulped down his whisky and stumped to the door. Mrs. Brockwell, with a shrug of her bare, thin shoulders, followed him, and Mr. Budd, feeling not a little embarrassed, lumbered heavily in their rear.

The meal was a good one, beautifully cooked and served, but neither Brockwell nor his wife ate much of it, and Mr. Budd was very glad when it was over. Tommy Custer announced that coffee was served in the drawing-room, but Mrs. Brockwell said that she didn't want any, and was going straight up to her room. She left them without a word.

'You married?' grunted Brockwell, as he and Mr. Budd made their way to the drawing-room, and the big man shook his head.

'Damn lucky feller,' said Brockwell. 'What a cow!'

Custer served coffee and withdrew, leaving them alone. Brockwell relapsed into a gloomy silence, and Mr. Budd was not sorry. It was quite impossible to carry on a normal conversation with the man. He had tried all kinds of subjects without arousing the slightest interest or any response but a grunt. A strange, uncouth man — and his money hadn't brought him very much happiness. Watching him through the poisonous smoke of one of his thin, black cigars, Mr. Budd wondered for the twentieth time where that money had come from. How had this illiterate boor, without charm, or any of the qualities necessary for a successful business man, succeeded in acquiring all his wealth? Maybe he had that queer money sense which some men possessed and which you either had or you hadn't. Mr. Budd thought, ruefully, that *he* hadn't. It was a kind of Midas touch which couldn't be acquired, and in most cases it seemed to be more of a curse than a blessing.

Just after nine o'clock it began to rain again; a heavy downpour that hissed monotonously. Henry Brockwell appeared to have fallen asleep in the big armchair, and Mr. Budd began to feel drowsy himself. In order to counteract this, he got up and went out into the hall.

Tom Custer appeared from the kitchen regions carrying a tray.

'Cocoa,' he said, disgustedly, in answer to Mr. Budd's questioning glance. '*She* wants it.' He jerked his head towards the staircase and the stout superintendent concluded he was referring to Mrs. Brockwell. As he began to ascend the stairs, Brockwell appeared at the open door of the drawing-room.

'What's that you've got? Where are you taking it?' he demanded, roughly.

'The missus wants it,' answered Custer.

'Come back here. *I'll* take it,' ordered Brockwell. 'I'm goin' up ter see her anyway . . . ' His face was flushed and his small eyes snapped angrily. Spoiling for another row, thought Mr. Budd. Nice, pleasant house to be in.

Custer relinquished the tray with alacrity, and Brockwell went up the stairs with it. Mr. Budd followed him slowly. Half-way up the man turned round.

'What are you coming for?' he asked, curtly.

'Doin' me job,' retorted Mr. Budd. 'I'm here to see that you don't come to no harm, an' I'm doin' it.'

'What 'arm do you think can come ter me in the 'ouse?' said Brockwell.

'I don't know, but I'm takin' no chances,' said Mr. Budd.

The man grunted and resumed his

journey. At Mrs. Brockwell's door he paused, turned the handle, and pushed it open. Going in he closed the door behind him and Mr. Budd, lingering in the corridor, heard Mrs. Brockwell's voice shrilly demanding to know what the hell he wanted. Brockwell's voice rumbled a reply and then the woman cried: 'You get out of 'ere, see,' and 'I'll go when I choose,' shouted Brockwell, and the next moment they were going at it hammer and tongs, hurling abuse at each other with increasing venom.

Mr. Budd couldn't hear all they said because sometimes they dropped their voices, but he heard enough to realize that the quarrel, which had been begun in the drawing-room, was being continued. For fifteen minutes it went on without cessation and then there was a crash of breaking china.

'You vicious bitch,' cried Brockwell. 'You might have cut me ter pieces. Put that blasted jug down, will yer . . . ?' There was another crash and Brockwell came quickly out of the door and slammed it behind him.

'I'll deal with yer ter-morrow,' he screamed, hoarse with rage, and Mr. Budd saw that he was dripping with cocoa. Mrs. Brockwell had, apparently, finished the argument by hurling the contents of the tray at him.

'She's dangerous,' he growled, mopping himself down with a handkerchief. 'One o' these days I'll give 'er such a beatin'-up she'll never forget it.' He glared malevolently at the closed door. 'Come along ter my room,' he said. 'I want ter talk ter you.'

Mr. Budd followed him along the corridor. His room was next to Mrs. Brockwell's and from the open doorway he could keep an eye on her door, provided he did not go inside the room. He explained this to Brockwell.

'All right, all right,' said Brockwell, impatiently. 'Yer needn't come into the room. I've got ter change this coat. It's soaked with 'er blasted cocoa.' He went on talking while he changed, and Mr. Budd leaned against the door frame. 'I've been thinkin' about this chap, Naylor,' he said, 'an' maybe there's somethin' in it. I wasn't ter blame, as I've told you, for his father's goin' ter gaol, but 'e may think I was, an' he may be out to revenge himself. That's what you think, ain't it?'

'It's a possibility,' answered Mr. Budd, cautiously.

'Those playin'-cards point ter 'im, don't they?' continued Brockwell, 'an' I can't think of anyone else it *could* be. It sounds a bit far-fetched, but there it is. Don't you think so?'

'Well,' remarked the big man, 'there's a lot in what you say . . .'

'P'raps,' said Brockwell, putting on a gaudy silk dressing-gown, 'that gal's in it too — Lake's daughter. They're related, ain't they? The more yer come ter think about it the more likely it seems . . .'

'Do you think they'd go to the lengths of killin' three people for the sake o' avenging two?' said Mr. Budd.

'Why not? It's 'appened before, ain't it?' said Brockwell. 'I wouldn't believe it when yer first told me, but after turnin' it over in me mind I've kinda come to think different. I don't think yer've got to look farther than them two . . .'

'You may be right,' murmured Mr. Budd, and he wondered what had induced this change of front. He had always thought that Brockwell had suspected Naylor in spite of the man's outward scepticism, but what had suddenly made him admit it? Could it be that his fear had got the better of him?

'I don't think I'll come down again,' said Brockwell, abruptly. 'I'll get ter bed instead. I s'pose you're goin' ter stop out there all night?'

'Until two o'clock,' said Mr. Budd, 'an' then Sergeant Leek'll take my place . . . '

'D'you think it's necessary?' asked Brockwell. ''ow could anythin' 'appen to us? Nobody can get near the 'ouse with that feller outside, can they? Why don't yer turn in?'

Mr. Budd shook his head.

'I'm takin' no chances,' he said, firmly. 'I don't see how anyone can get in, but they might, an' I'm not riskin' that might.'

'Well, 'ave it yer own way,' grunted Brockwell, brusquely. 'I'm goin' ter bed. Good night.'

'Good night,' said Mr. Budd, and he

moved away as the other shut the door almost in his face. There was a chair midway between the two bedroom doors and on this he sat himself wearily. A glance at his watch told him that it was a quarter to ten. Four hours and a quarter to go before he would see his bed. It seemed a dickens of a long time, and he was already feeling tired. If he'd had any sense he'd have had a sleep during the afternoon . . . He heard the stairs creak and looking round saw Tommy Custer appear with a tray.

' 'ere's some cawfee,' said the little man. 'I'm just orf ter bed.'

Mr. Budd took the cup and saucer gratefully.

'Yer're a lucky feller,' he remarked.

'Don't know why yer don't 'it the 'ay yerself,' said Mr. Custer, tucking the empty tray under his arm. 'Perishin' waste o' time sittin' there, that's what it is. What d'you think can 'appen to 'em?'

'What happened to James?' said Mr. Budd, meaningly.

'That was different.' Mr. Custer made a hideous grimace. 'There wasn't a 'busy' walkin' round and round the 'ouse then. H'anybody coulda got in . . . '

'In case anybody gets in now, I'm the second line of defence.' Mr. Budd took a gulp of hot coffee and burnt his tongue.

'If somebody bumped 'em both orf *I* wouldn't lose no sleep,' said Tommy Custer candidly. 'Blimey! Wot a pair! Always spittin' and scratching at each other like a couple o' cats.' He shook his head. 'When can I sling me 'ook?' he said. 'I'm fed up with this job an' that's a fact.'

'Not yet, Tommy,' answered Mr. Budd. 'Not until everythin's over an' in the bag. An' then, if you've got nuthin' ter do with it, you can go where and when you like . . . '

'If I've got nuthin' . . . ? 'ere, wot are you talking about?' Mr. Custer's pinched face was anxious. 'You don't think I 'ave, do yer? Cor blimey!'

'I've got ter *know* you 'aven't, Tommy, before I can let you go wanderin' off,' said Mr. Budd, gently. 'An' I can't know that until I find out who has. So I'm afraid you'll just 'ave ter stay put for a bit.'

'But look 'ere . . . ' began Mr. Custer.

'It's no good arguin',' interrupted Mr. Budd. 'That's . . . '

He broke off and leapt to his feet as a loud report came from behind the closed door of Mrs. Brockwell's room.

'Blimey, wot was that?' exclaimed the startled Mr. Custer, dropping the tray with a clatter.

'It sounded like a shot,' grunted Mr. Budd, in alarm, and he was at the door with surprising agility for so stout a man. Turning the handle he flung the door open. The shaded lights were on and the air was heavy with the smell of burnt cordite. On the floor, in the middle of the room, lay Mrs. Brockwell in a crumpled heap, and above her drifted a sluggish streak of blue-grey smoke.

Mr. Budd's incredulous eyes saw the red stain on the back of her cream negligee and — something else that lay near her outflung arm . . . A crumpled playing-card — the King of Diamonds.

Part Four

The King of Diamonds

1

Mr. Budd stared into the lighted room in utter stupefaction, too astonished for a second or two to do anything else . . .

'Cor blimey, 'ow did it 'appen?' whispered the horrified Tom Custer at his elbow, and the question jerked him out of his bewildered trance and his training reasserted itself.

'Go an' telephone ter Doctor Middlesham,' he ordered. 'Tell 'im to come 'ere right away. An' when you've done that go outside and find Sergeant Mackleberry . . . '

'Is she . . . dead?' breathed Custer, staring at the motionless form of the woman on the floor in fascinated awe.

'I don' know . . . I think so,' said Mr. Budd. 'Do as I tell yer, will you?'

'She must 'ave shot 'erself,' said Custer, huskily. 'She couldn't 'ave bin . . . '

'What the 'ell was that noise?' Brockwell came out of his room clad in pyjamas, his hair ruffled and a scowl on his unprepossessing face. 'What's goin' on, hey?'

'There's been an accident,' replied Mr. Budd, quickly. 'Somethin's happened to your wife . . . No, stay where you are, please,' he added, sharply, as Brockwell took a step towards him.

'An accident . . . ? God Almighty, you don't mean . . . ? What's 'appened to 'er?' Brockwell stammered incoherently, with a dawning fear in his small eyes.

'I think she's shot herself. I don't know yet . . . ' said Mr. Budd. 'Go an' do what I told yer, Custer, an' get a move on . . . '

Tom Custer dragged his eyes away from the spectacle beyond the open door and, turning, hurried away down the stairs.

'Shot 'erself?' muttered Brockwell. 'Shot 'erself . . . ?' His mouth sagged loosely and all the bluster seemed to ooze out of him. He sat down suddenly on the chair, which Mr. Budd had so recently occupied, and dropped his head in his hands.

The stout superintendent went cautiously into the room and stooped over

Mrs. Brockwell. It didn't take him long to assure himself that she was dead. Her eyes were open and already glazing, and the polished back of his watch remained undimmed when he held it close to her parted lips. He looked round for the weapon from which the shot had been fired, but he couldn't see it. Unless it was under the body, it wasn't there. But, of course, it *must* be under the body. He couldn't move that to look until after the doctor had made his examination, but he could take it for granted that it was there. It couldn't be anywhere else in the room and it must be still in the room. This was a case of suicide, not murder. Murder was completely out of the question this time. There could not have been anyone else in the room except Mrs. Brockwell. *That* was definite, anyway. The window was shut and fastened; nobody could have come or gone that way. And he himself had been watching the door, so that was equally impossible . . . No, it was suicide all right. For some reason Mrs. Brockwell had shot herself, though it was a queer place to have chosen to do it — just under her shoulder-blades . . . Difficult, too, getting her arm in that position . . . And the playing-card . . . Why had she put *that* there?

Mr. Budd stood motionless, looking slowly around the room, and he began to feel an acute uneasiness gradually steal over him. There was something wrong, somewhere . . . He took out his hand-kerchief, covered his hand with it, and went over to a large wardrobe. The door was unlocked and he opened it carefully and looked inside. It was full of clothes, but nothing else. Nobody was concealed within. He stooped and peered under the bed. Nobody there either. He straight-ened up, slowly expelling his pent-up breath. It *must* have been suicide. There was no possible place in the room, other than the wardrobe, or under the bed, where anyone could have concealed themselves; no means by which they could have got out after firing the shot . . . No, it must have been suicide, in spite of the fact that she had chosen such an awkward way of doing it . . . And why had she done it? Some sort of sudden brain-storm possibly. She was the type of woman who might go suddenly all unbalanced . . .

He moved back to the open doorway, avoiding the broken china that lay just inside, and leaning against the frame he thoughtfully surveyed the room. Although he kept assuring himself that it must be suicide, he was vaguely dissatisfied . . .

The sound of footsteps on the stairs made him turn quickly. Mr. Custer, followed by Sergeant Mackleberry, appeared and came towards him.

'The doctor's comin' at once,' said the little man, breathlessly. 'Cor blimey! 'e wasn't 'alf surprised when I told 'im wot 'ad 'appened . . . '

'Is it true, sir?' broke in Mackleberry. 'Has Mrs. Brockwell shot 'erself?'

'Well, that's what it looks like,' said Mr. Budd, a trifle doubtfully. 'We 'eard the shot, an' I was at the door an' 'ad it open in less than a minute. I don't see 'ow it could be anythin' else . . . '

'Nobody come near the house from outside, sir,' said Mackleberry. 'I'll take me oath on that . . . '

'If they 'ad they couldn't have got into 'er room,' said Mr. Budd. 'An' even if they'd got in there earlier, an' 'id themselves, they couldn't have got out . . . It's just *got* ter be suicide, unless we're up against a murderer who can make himself invisible.'

And that's just what he had to admit, later, that they were up against, for when Doctor Middlesham arrived he stated definitely that the wound could *not* have been self-inflicted. And there was no weapon concealed under the body.

2

'It's impossible, that's what it is,' said Mr. Budd. 'Just downright, completely, an' utterly impossible.'

He looked weary and drawn, and his eyelids were heavy and puffy. It was nearly two hours since he had made the incredible discovery, and during the ensuing period he had been a very busy man indeed. A telephone call to Bedlington had routed Superintendent Tidworthy out of his comfortable bed and brought him post-haste to The Croft, accompanied by Major Toppington, whom he had called for on his way. They were now gathered in the big drawing-room refreshing themselves with hot coffee, hastily prepared by the excited Mr. Custer. Henry Brockwell had completely broken down under the shock of his wife's death and been given a sedative by Middlesham. He was now sleeping heavily in his bed.

While he waited for the arrival of

Tidworthy, Mr. Budd had made a thorough examination of the dead woman's room. Beyond the window and the door there was no other means of getting in or out, and yet somebody had succeeded in doing both. There was no longer any doubt that it was murder. The complete absence of any weapon was sufficient to prove that, without Middlesham's assertion that it was physically impossible for Mrs. Brockwell to have inflicted the wound herself. And the shot which had killed her had been fired at close range. There were powder marks and singeing on her negligee. How the murderer had managed to get away during the few seconds that elapsed between Mr. Budd hearing the shot and opening the door, was an inexplicable mystery.

'You're absolutely certain that no one could have slipped out of that room while your back was turned?' said the Chief Constable, and Mr. Budd shook his head.

'Me back was never turned long enough,' he answered. 'I never 'ad my eyes off that door from the time I 'eard the shot until after I'd searched the room thoroughly an 'proved that it was empty. It's the gettin' out what's so puzzlin'. I can imagine that somebody might 'ave got in durin' the evenin', or some part of the day, an' 'id themselves under the bed, or in that wardrobe, but 'ow the hell they got out again is beyond me.'

'Well, there must be *some* reasonable explanation,' said Major Toppington. 'The age of miracles is past — that kind of miracle, anyhow. People can't wrap themselves in an invisible cloak or fly up the chimney on a broomstick. Somebody shot that woman in that room and got away afterwards. What we've got to do is to find out how.'

'Yes, sir,' murmured Mr. Budd. He looked at Leek, perched on the arm of an easy chair, and from him to Tidworthy, sitting on the settee, frowning and gently rubbing his bald head.

'There's no possibility of there being another way into the room, I suppose?' went on the Chief Constable, pacing up and down. 'A secret door, something like that, I mean?'

'I don't think so, sir,' said Mr. Budd. 'I did look for anything of the sort, an' I asked Brockwell. He'd never heard of one, an' 'e had the house built.'

'What about the window?' suggested Tidworthy. 'Are you quite sure a strong, agile man couldn't have slipped out that way?'

'The winder was shut an' fastened on the inside,' remarked Mr. Budd, wearily. 'You can wash that out . . .'

'The chimney,' exclaimed Leek, suddenly. 'I'll bet *that's* it . . .'

'There ain't no chimney,' broke in Mr. Budd, giving him a withering glare. 'The room's 'eated by an electric fire built into the wall. If you didn't go about with yer eyes shut, you'd 'ave known that.'

'Oh, is it?' muttered the abashed sergeant, weakly, and he was silent.

'So that we're left with the door,' said Major Toppington. 'What was it Sherlock Holmes used to say? 'Eliminate the impossible and *whatever* remains, however improbable, must be the truth.' I always thought there was a lot of sense in that, you know . . .'

'If you eliminate the impossible from this business there ain't *nuthin*' left,' grunted Mr. Budd.

There was a complete silence. The truth of his statement was so obvious that nobody could refute it.

'You know,' said the Chief Constable, suddenly, 'there's going to be an almighty uproar over this.'

Mr. Budd nodded. He *did* know. He would have to face an irate Assistant Commissioner and try to explain how he had failed to a man who would listen to no explanation . . .

'It's ridiculous,' exclaimed Superintendent Tidworthy, irritably. 'If a thing happens, there must be a *way* it could happen . . . '

'I agree with you,' assented Major Toppington. 'There's something we've missed. Now let's go over everything carefully and see if we can find it.'

They did so, checking every moment of that eventful evening, but they could find no loophole. When they had finished they stared at each other.

'It *is* impossible,' grunted the Chief

Constable. 'It *couldn't* have happened . . . '

'Only it *did* happen, sir,' said Tidworthy.

'An' there's one more card left to complete the flush,' remarked Mr. Budd, under his breath. 'The Ace o' Diamonds . . . '

'Brockwell?' said Major Toppington.

'Yes, 'e's the last, an' 'e knows it,' said the big man. 'That's why 'e's broken down. You don't s'pose it was grief over his wife, do yer? He's 'alf dead, already, with fear . . . '

'We've *got* to protect him,' said the Chief Constable, incisively. 'We've got to . . . '

'We tried to protect James an' Mrs. Brockwell,' said Mr. Budd, 'an' we failed . . . '

'Well, we mustn't fail a third time,' declared Major Toppington, curtly. 'We've got to find the murderer before he can strike again . . . '

3

There was no sleep for Mr. Budd that night. When the photographer had finished his job, the body of Mrs. Brockwell removed, the death room sealed up, and Tidworthy and the Chief Constable had gone, he went wearily up to his room and lay down on the bed. It was nearly two o'clock and raining heavily but, although he felt tired, he had no intention of allowing himself to sleep. His reputation was at stake. In some way or other he must retrieve the failure of the night, and before he had to come up in front of Colonel Blair. Once he was taken off the case it would be too late. Although it was absurd to suppose that the murderer would strike again so soon, he had insisted that Leek should keep a guard over Henry Brockwell for the remainder of the night and, this time, not from outside the door, but at the sleeping man's bedside.

Propped up against the pillows, with a

cigar between his teeth, Mr. Budd tried to flog his brain into activity. There was bound to be an answer to his problem if only he could get on the right track. Up to now he had been stumbling about in a dark maze; wasting his time up innumerable little side alleys that ended abruptly in blank walls. The right path — the main path — that would lead him to the welcome light, *must* be close at hand.

With his eyes half closed he forced himself to concentrate. Detail by detail he went carefully over the actual facts concerning the murders, and when he had got these, clearly and concisely in their right order — and very few they were, he decided ruefully — he began to examine them in relation to the people connected with the case.

Quite obviously Roger Naylor and Harriet Lake were the chief suspects. Antrim was a possible one, but the other two had a stronger motive. Antrim, so far as was known, had only been concerned with Sandra Brockwell, and the leaving of the playing-cards would have had no significance for him, whereas they would have the greatest possible significance for Roger Naylor. Brockwell, if the story of the cheque were true, had been responsible for the disgrace and ultimate death of Naylor's father and, indirectly, for the death of his mother. It was quite conceivable that an impressionable boy could have been imbued with such a hatred for the man who had broken up his home that he would revenge himself when the opportunity arose. And the opportunity had arisen when Brockwell had come to live at Long Millford. It was also conceivable that Harriet Lake, also hating the man, and for practically the same reason, would have been prepared to help in any scheme of revenge that Naylor might suggest. In fact, it was possible that *Harriet Lake* had been the first to suggest it. There was nothing of the 'clinging vine' type about her, and Mr. Budd could very easily imagine her as the prime mover, even in a matter of murder. If it had been *Brockwell* who had been murdered, he would not have looked any further than those two, but his mind boggled at making them responsible for wholesale slaughter. Whatever Brockwell had done, his children could not have had anything to do with it, and he could not bring himself to believe that Harriet Lake, or Roger Naylor, would have killed them, even as an indirect means of punishing their father. Killing the family off one by one and leaving Brockwell until the last was a refined method of torture that, he was sure, would never have occurred to them and, even if it had, they would never have put it into practice.

But, eliminating Naylor and Harriet Lake, left him with Antrim. And Antrim had no possible motive, except in the case of Sandra Brockwell . . .

His cigar had gone out and he reached for the matches and relit it. Who else was there? Doctor Middlesham, Clarissa Pipp-Partington, Sir Oswald Pipp-Partington, Middlesham's sister — what was her name? — Rita, that was it, and Tommy Custer. Well, what about Custer? He was a known crook, and if it had been a case of burglary there wouldn't have been any question, but Mr. Budd couldn't see him as a murderer; and, besides, again he had no motive.

That was the vital thing — the motive. If once he could discover a motive that would supply *someone* with a strong and plausible reason for wanting the whole Brockwell family dead, then everything would be easy . . .

He punched the pillows to make them softer, and settled himself more comfortably. Now what motive *would* cover that? The answer came instantly. Gain. If all the Brockwells were dead, who got the money? Henry Brockwell could tell him that. It was probably a relation. If it was a man, and he possessed any of the attributes of Brockwell, Mr. Budd could well imagine that a murder, more or less, would not worry him if, by that means, he was going to get hold of a lot of money. There was definitely something here; a motive that was solid and understandable. But why the playing-cards? They had to be fitted in and explained.

Mr. Budd's brows drew together. Supposing, after all, they were just trimmings; red herrings to distract the attention from the *real* truth? There might be a lot in that. He had always thought they were too much like something out of a book. This supposed relative of Brockwell's would, presumably, have known all about the Naylor affair. Supposing, when he had planned the series of murders, that he had *also* known that Naylor's *son* was living in the district. What was more likely than that he would attempt to throw suspicion on him?

The big man felt his depression lifting a little. He was getting somewhere — not very far, but somewhere. This was more of a coherent pattern than he had yet achieved. It was true that it did *not* explain the impossible killing of Mrs. Brockwell, but it was something a great deal more tangible than he had yet evolved . . .

The first thing to do was to tackle Brockwell and find out who got the money. Everything depended on that. He wished that he could do that at once, but Brockwell would still be sleeping off the effects of the drug which Middlesham had given him. It would have to wait until the morning . . .

He yawned, and suddenly realized how tired he was. But he had made a little headway. It was not much, but it was further than he had got before . . .

He hoisted himself wearily off the bed, undressed, and was soon back in it, fast asleep.

4

He was wakened by the arrival of Custer with a cup of tea. The little man's face was drawn and pinched and his eyes were red-rimmed from lack of sleep.

'Wasser time?' asked Mr. Budd, huskily, blinking up at him.

''alf-past eight,' answered Custer. 'Cor blimey, wot a night, eh? Me eyes feels like two burnt 'oles in a blanket . . . '

'Didn't you get any sleep?' said Mr. Budd, struggling up in the bed and taking the tea.

'Sleep?' echoed Tommy Custer. 'Fat lot of chawnce there was for any sleep in this blinkin' 'ouse. I lay down fer a couple of hours, that's all . . . '

'Why, what kept you up?' demanded the big man, sipping his tea.

'That there Bleecher woman,' answered Mr. Custer, disgustedly. 'Carryin' on somethink awful, she was. Gawd knows what woke 'er up, but nuthin' 'ud get her back ter bed. I don't know what you're goin' ter do fer any food ter-day, 'cos she's packed her things an' she swears she's goin'. She says all the money in China ain't goin' to get her to stay in the 'ouse another hour . . . '

'She can't do that,' said Mr. Budd, firmly. 'Where is she now?'

' 'avin' a cuppa tea in the kitchen, an' waitin' fer a cab ter take 'er, an' 'er things, to Bedlington,' said Mr. Custer. 'Cor blimey, what a cow! Not that I blames 'er . . . '

'I'll come an' talk to her,' declared Mr. Budd, decisively. He gulped down the remainder of the hot tea, got out of bed, and pulled on a dressing-gown. 'What about Brockwell? Is he up?'

Mr. Custer shook his head.

'No,' he replied. 'He still looks dopey to me. I took 'im, and that sergeant feller, a cuppa tea just now. The old man drank it, but he weren't properly awake. Sort o' 'alf dazed like . . . '

'Make 'im some really strong coffee,' said Mr. Budd, thrusting his feet into his slippers. 'I want ter talk to that feller.

277

Let's go down.' He followed Mr. Custer down the stairs to the kitchen.

Mrs. Bleecher, fully dressed and wearing a rather rakish hat perched on her head, was sitting at the table drinking a cup of tea, and surrounded by a large assortment of bags and parcels. She surveyed Mr. Budd with a truculent glare.

'An' what may *you* want?' she demanded, rudely. 'I'm not answerin' any questions. I was in bed an' asleep an' I don't know nuthink, an' don't *want* to know nuthink. The goin's on in this 'ouse is somethink I'd rather not be mixed up in, an' I'm goin' . . . '

'I'm afraid, ma'am,' interrupted Mr. Budd, politely, 'that you can't go yet . . . '

'Ho, an' who's goin' ter stop me?' inquired Mrs. Bleecher.

'Well, if it becomes necessary, *I* shall, ma'am,' answered Mr. Budd. 'You see . . . '

'Are you suggestin',' said Mrs. Bleecher, 'that I am under arrest?'

'No, no,' said Mr. Budd, reassuringly. 'Nothin' so drastic as that, ma'am . . . '

'I'm very glad to 'ear it,' said Mrs. Bleecher, tossing her head, and very nearly jerking off her hat in the process. 'Because if anybody starts tryin' to arrest *me*, there's goin' ter be a lot o' trouble. I'm a respectable woman, I am, an' I'm not agoin' to have my character defamed by no one, p'lice or no p'lice . . . '

'Nobody would dream of doin' such a thing,' said Mr. Budd, diplomatically.

'I'm very glad to 'ear it,' declared Mrs. Bleecher again.

'But you must realize,' he continued, quickly, 'that a murder was committed in this 'ouse last night an' . . . '

'*That's* why I'm goin',' said Mrs. Bleecher. 'I told Mr. Custer that if there was any more murders I should go, an' I'm goin'.'

She looked at Tommy Custer as though defying him to dispute this statement.

'That's all very well, ma'am,' said Mr. Budd, patiently. 'But what I'm tryin' to tell you is that *nobody* can leave the 'ouse until the p'lice give their permission . . . '

'Ho, indeed?' Mrs. Bleecher visibly swelled with indignation. 'H'is this, or is it not, a free country? Just let me tell you that I'm goin' when I want to, an' that's as soon as the keb comes for me. Now *you* try an' stop me!'

Mr. Budd was a little disconcerted. He had the power to detain this belligerent woman, but he was reluctant to use it. It would be tantamount to arresting her, and he did not want to go to such an extreme if it could be avoided.

'I can understand 'ow you feel about it, ma'am,' he said, in his most conciliatory manner. 'It's very unpleasant an' disturbin' for a lady in your position, but we'd be very much obliged if you'd stay 'ere until after the inquest. I don't think there'll be any objection, then, to your doin' as you like.'

'Why should I 'ave to stay?' asked Mrs. Bleecher, slightly mollified by this way of putting it.

'Well, yer see,' said Mr. Budd, following up his advantage with great cunning, 'it's the usual thing in a case o' this kind. I remember 'avin' to explain the same thing ter the Duchess of Spenmoor. 'er grace wanted ter pack up an' leave Spenmoor Castle direc'ly after the duke was murdered an' I 'ad ter be very firm with 'er — very firm indeed.' He had invented the whole thing on the spur of the moment, hoping that the obviously rather snobbish Mrs. Bleecher would swallow it. She did.

'Of course,' she said, with great dignity, 'h'if it's a question of doin' one's duty, I 'ope I knows what's expected of me. Mixin', as I always 'ave, with some o' the best people in the land . . .'

'Quite, ma'am,' said Mr. Budd, hastily. 'I was sure you'd understand if it was put to yer in the proper way.'

'You can rely h'on me,' said Mrs. Bleecher, graciously, 'ter be 'ere when wanted, though bein' of a sensitized nature, an' always was from a child, the h'atmosphere is irksome.'

'I'm sure I'm very much obliged to you,' said Mr. Budd, privately heartily agreeing with Tom Custer's terse, but vulgar description of the lady.

He went back upstairs, had a bath, shaved and dressed. Apparently Mrs. Bleecher had not only consented to stay, but had resumed her duties, for, when he came down again, there was a pleasant smell of coffee and he found breakfast laid for him in the dining-room. Mrs. Bleecher had taken the behaviour of the mythical Duchess of Spenmoor as a pattern.

The big man ate his breakfast without his usual enjoyment. The responsibilities of his position weighed heavily upon him and, although he felt better than he had done in the early hours of the morning, he was still a greatly worried and troubled man.

When he had finished the meal he went in search of Leek. The lean detective was dozing in a chair beside Henry Brockwell's bed and blinked sleepily at Mr. Budd when he came in.

'Go an' have yer breakfast an' then get off ter bed,' said his superior. 'You can sleep until two o'clock this afternoon an' then I shall want yer.'

'Two o'clock?' echoed Leek, plaintively. 'That ain't long. I've got a lot o' sleep ter make up . . . '

'Make it up in yer spare time,' snapped Mr. Budd. 'Now get along.'

Leek went, muttering aggrievedly under his breath, and the stout superintendent looked at the sleeping man. Brockwell was breathing heavily and regularly and his eyes were closed, but Mr. Budd was certain that he was not asleep. He sat down in the chair which Leek had vacated and watched the man under drooping eyelids.

Presently Brockwell stirred and opened his eyes.

'Hello,' he muttered, thickly. 'What are you doin' 'ere?'

'Waitin' for you ter wake up, Mr. Brockwell,' said Mr. Budd. ''ow d'you feel now?'

'Feel? . . . I'm all right . . . ' Brockwell lifted himself on to one elbow. 'I want a drink . . . Get me a drink, will you? There's whisky and a glass in that cupboard . . . ' He nodded towards a cupboard in one corner of the room.

Mr. Budd got up, went over, and came back with a half-full bottle of Johnnie Walker and a glass. Brockwell grabbed them eagerly, poured out half a tumbler of neat whisky and drank it at a gulp.

'That's better,' he gasped. ''ave some?'

Mr. Budd shook his head.

'Please yerself,' said Brockwell. He

poured out another four fingers and put the bottle down on the bed-side table. 'Is . . . have they . . . taken 'er away?' he asked.

'Yes,' answered Mr. Budd.

'It's awful . . . terrible,' muttered Brockwell. 'John an' James, Sandra an' Helen . . . all in a few weeks . . . I'm leavin' this place . . . I'm packin' up an' I'm goin' . . . while the goin's good . . . ' He swallowed half of the second drink.

'I'm afraid you won't be able ter go yet, Mr. Brockwell,' said Mr. Budd.

'Why not?' Brockwell glared at him resentfully. 'D'you think I'm going ter stop 'ere an' be murdered . . . ?'

'I'll see you ain't murdered,' began Mr. Budd, and the other interrupted him with a harsh laugh.

'You'll see?' he repeated, scornfully. 'Ruddy lot of good *you* are . . . '

'I'll guarantee that no 'arm'll come to you while you're here,' said Mr. Budd, suppressing his annoyance at the insult because he felt that there was some justification for it.

'Same as you looked after 'elen an'

James, I s'pose?' sneered Brockwell. 'You fellers from Scotland Yard ain't any better'n what the locals are, an' they're a dud lot . . . '

'The fact remains,' said Mr. Budd, quietly, 'that you'll 'ave to remain here until after the inquiry is over, or until such time as you receive permission ter leave.'

Brockwell's face flushed to a darker red, but he said mildly: 'Oh, well, if I've got ter, I've got ter.' He drained his whisky. ''ave yer found out anythin'?' he asked.

'Nuthin' fresh,' admitted Mr. Budd. 'I'd like to ask you some questions, Mr. Brockwell, which may have some bearin' on the matter. Have you made a will?'

Brockwell looked startled.

'Yes,' he answered. 'What the devil 'as that got . . . ?'

'Who benefits in the event of your death?'

'My . . . my wife would have got half, an' 'alf would 'ave been divided among the children . . . '

''ow much would that amount to, roughly?'

Brockwell frowned and considered.

'Somewhere round about two 'undred an' fifty thousand quid, I s'pose,' he replied, slowly, and Mr. Budd pursed his lips. It was a large sum of money, he thought: a sufficient inducement for someone to have committed four murders, and be prepared to commit a fifth, to acquire it . . .

'An' who would get this money, now,' he said, aloud, 'if anythin' 'appened to you?'

'I s'pose it 'ud go ter my sister,' answered Brockwell, thoughtfully. 'She'd be next of kin . . . '

'Where is she?' asked Mr. Budd, quickly, and Brockwell shook his head.

'I dunno,' he declared. 'I ain't seen or 'eard of 'er for years — not since she married . . . '

'Who did she marry?' asked the big man, ungrammatically.

Brockwell puckered up his mouth and scratched one of his eyebrows.

'Now, lemme see,' he muttered. 'Classy chap 'e was, but I'm damned if I can remember 'is name. Began with a T, I think, but I couldn't be sure. It's nearly twenty years ago, now . . . '

The usually phlegmatic Mr. Budd felt a stirring of excitement in his veins.

'Try an' think,' he urged. 'It may be important . . . '

'Why?' demanded Brockwell. 'I can't see where all this is gettin' us . . . '

'Can't you?' said Mr. Budd. 'Well, I'll tell yer. I'm lookin' fer a motive — a good, substantial motive — for somebody wantin' to kill off all of yer. An' two 'undred an' fifty thousand pounds is the most substantial one I've found up ter now . . . '

Henry Brockwell gaped at him. A variety of expressions chased themselves over his face. Surprise, incredulity, doubt . . . 'I thought this feller Naylor was . . . ' he began.

'Naylor's motive ain't strong,' broke in Mr. Budd. 'At least it ain't strong enough to satisfy me . . . '

'What about them cards?' said Brockwell. 'Who else could 'ave left them . . . ?'

'Anybody who knew the story an' wanted to throw suspicion on Naylor,' retorted Mr. Budd. 'Now d'yer see what I mean?'

Apparently Brockwell saw very well. Apprehension replaced the other transient expressions and remained.

'My God!' he whispered, and he seemed to have a momentary difficulty in getting his breath. 'Edie would never . . . do anythin' like that . . . '

'Maybe *she* wouldn't,' said Mr. Budd, guessing that he was referring to his sister, 'but this 'usband of hers might . . . '

'I wish I could remember 'is name,' muttered Brockwell. 'Everard somethin' or other. I'm sure it began with a T . . . '

'Where was yer sister married?' asked the big man.

'Canada — Ontario,' said Brockwell.

'The records 'ud show who she married,' said Mr. Budd. 'You say you 'aven't seen or heard anythin' of 'er for nearly twenty years?'

'That's right,' agreed Brockwell. 'We didn't 'it it off too well, Edie an' me. She allus thought she was a cut above me, an' when she met this feller . . . Dammit, *what* was 'is name . . . ?'

'So you wouldn't know but what your sister an' 'er husband might be in

England,' continued Mr. Budd, pursuing his original line of thought, 'or even in *this* district?'

'You're right there,' agreed Brockwell. He answered mechanically, his mind quite evidently thinking of something else. Mr. Budd saw that his suggestion had obviously upset him. He was disturbed and worried — much more so than he had been before.

'Twenty years is a long time,' went on the fat detective, stroking his nose. 'People 'ud alter a lot in that time, wouldn't they? An' you never knew this feller really well . . . '

'No . . . no, I never knew 'im well . . . ' Brockwell answered, absently, and added under his breath: 'My God!'

''ave you got a photograph of your sister?' asked Mr. Budd, and the other shook his head.

'On'y as a kid,' he answered. 'Crawlin' on the 'earthrug. That wouldn't be much use to you . . . ' He reached over and poured himself out another drink. 'This idea of yours 'as given me a bit of a shock,' he said, taking a big gulp of whisky. 'I'd like ter be alone an' think it over . . . '

'Sorry, Mr. Brockwell, but that's impossible,' said Mr. Budd. 'From now on, till this affair's cleared up, there's got ter be somebody always with you. Either me, or Sergeant Leek, or Sergeant Mackleberry. I'm not riskin' any more killin's . . . '

'But 'ow can anyone get at me 'ere?' protested Brockwell. 'It's impossible . . . '

'It was 'impossible' with Mrs. Brockwell,' said Mr. Budd. 'But they did it all the same . . . '

5

Brockwell argued, but the big man was adamant. He stayed with the other until eleven o'clock, when Sergeant Mackleberry arrived and took his place. He brought with him the reports from the men who had been keeping Roger Naylor under observation. Naylor had spent the early part of the previous evening with Harriet Lake. At eight-thirty he had left the cottage and returned home to Bedlington and, so far as the watchers could testify, had remained there. Mr. Budd realized that this was not conclusive. The detective had been watching the front of the house, and if Naylor had had any idea that he was being kept under observation, and had wished to leave without being seen, he would probably have found a way to get out at the back.

He put through a call to the Yard, requesting that a cable should be sent to Ontario asking for all available information concerning the marriage of Edie, or

Edith, Brockwell with a man unknown, and gave the approximate date. He asked that the matter should be treated with the utmost urgency and, when this had been attended to, was put through to the Assistant Commissioner.

The next twenty minutes was the most unpleasant period in the big man's life. Colonel Blair listened in silence to what he had to say and then let himself go. Mr. Budd's face grew redder and redder as the clipped voice proceeded.

'I quite agree with all you've just said, sir,' he replied, when the Assistant Commissioner had exhausted himself, 'an' I'm not makin' any excuses. All I can say is that if you'll give me another four days, I'll 'ave the murderer under lock an' key . . . ' He had not meant to make such a rash statement, and he only realized what he had said after it was out.

'Is that definite?' barked Colonel Blair. 'Can you guarantee that?'

Mr. Budd hesitated, and then burned his boats.

'Yes, sir,' he said, recklessly.

'Very well,' said the Assistant Commissioner.

'In view of your exceptionally good record, I'll give you another four days. But remember, if there are no results at the end of that time, you'll be recalled and I shall put another man on the case.'

'Very good, sir,' said Mr. Budd, and there was a click as Colonel Blair rang off. The big man got up from the telephone and wiped his perspiring face. Well, he'd done it now, he thought, ruefully. In four days' time he had to produce the murderer, or have the case taken out of his hands, with the consequent black mark on his sheet. What *had* induced him to make such a wild statement? Not that it made very much difference. If he hadn't promised something of the sort, Blair would have recalled him at once — at least he had four days in which to try and retrieve his failure.

Mr. Custer accosted him excitedly as he came into the hall.

''ere, I've found somethin',' said the little man. 'Come along an' I'll show yer.'

He led the way up the stairs to the landing above that from which Henry

Brockwell's, and Mrs. Brockwell's, bedrooms opened. In a corner was a huge linen cupboard, and Tom Custer opened the door.

'Look in there,' he cried, dramatically. 'On the floor . . . '

Mr. Budd looked. The floor was covered with the marks of muddy footprints. Lumps of dried mud, with grass still adhering to them, were scattered about. Somebody had come in from outside and stood in the cupboard for a considerable time.

'Yer see?' said Mr. Custer, triumphantly. 'That's where the feller what killed Mrs. Brockwell hid 'isself. Them marks wasn't there yesterday mornin'. I'll take me dyin' oath on that. I come 'ere ter get some clean towels an' there wasn't no sign of 'em . . . '

'What time did yer get the towels?' asked Mr. Budd.

'Round about 'leven o'clock,' said Mr. Custer.

'Wasn't the cupboard kept locked?'

'No. Yer twist this little brass thin', that's all.'

Mr. Budd rubbed his chin. Somebody had definitely concealed themselves in the cupboard, but it didn't explain how they had got into Mrs. Brockwell's bedroom, shot her, and got out again without being seen.

'Yer see wot 'appened?' said Mr. Custer. 'This feller sneaks into the 'ouse some time durin' the day, 'ides in 'ere, an' then, when the coast's clear, slips down an' 'ides 'isself in Mrs. Brockwell's bedroom. I'll bet 'e was there all the evenin'. It's as clear as clear . . . '

'An' then 'e shoots 'er an' vanishes into thin air,' grunted Mr. Budd. 'It's as clear as *mud*!'

'Well, any'ow, we know where 'e 'id,' said Mr. Custer. 'That's somethink, ain't it?'

'I'd rather know where he *went*,' retorted Mr. Budd. 'I'm goin' ter seal this cupboard, so if yer want anythin' out of it you'd better get it now.'

Tom Custer selected several articles, and the big man found some string and sealing-wax and sealed up the door.

'I'm holdin' you responsible to see that

that ain't opened,' he said, when his task was completed. 'That may be an important piece of evidence.'

He got out his car, drove over to Bedlington, and had an interview with the Chief Constable. Major Toppington agreed that his new theory was a plausible one.

'But you're going to have the deuce of a job bringing it home to these people,' he said. 'Even if you succeed in finding them in England, there isn't a scrap of real evidence against them. The fact that they come into the money isn't enough on its own . . . '

'I realize that, sir,' said Mr. Budd. 'But once we've found 'em, the evidence may come to light. If one of 'em did these murders 'e — I should say it was the 'usband — must 'ave been in the district on each occasion. If we can prove *that*, it would go a long way . . . '

'Yes,' said the Chief Constable, nodding. 'But don't forget the most important thing — you've got to show how the murder of Mrs. Brockwell was carried out. Until you can do that no jury would bring in a conviction.'

Mr. Budd told him of Tom Custer's discovery.

'It doesn't 'elp very much, I know, sir,' he ended. 'But it does prove that there was somebody 'idin' in the house that night.'

'The difficulty isn't how anyone got in,' said Major Toppington, echoing Mr. Budd's own words, 'but how they succeeded in getting out of that room after the murder. I think it's quite reasonable to suppose that they hid there, probably in the wardrobe, earlier in the day, when the room was empty. In fact, I'm pretty sure that that is what actually happened. But how the devil did they get out?'

Since Mr. Budd could think of no plausible explanation, he left the question unanswered.

On the way back to Long Millford, he decided to call on Harriet Lake. One end of Mill Lane came out into the Bedlington road and he turned the car into it. The surface was bad and he had to drive slowly. As he came in sight of the cottage, a man came out of the gate, got on a bicycle and pedalled rapidly away in the direction of the village. Mr. Budd only caught a glimpse of him, but that glimpse was enough. It was Tom Custer!

6

Why had Tom Custer been visiting Harriet Lake? thought the big man, as he watched the figure of the cyclist disappear round the bend. There might be nothing in it, of course, but on the other hand there might be a great deal . . .

He pulled up at the cottage gate and got heavily out of the car. Harriet opened the door in answer to his knock and he thought she looked a little disconcerted when she saw who it was.

'Oh, it's you,' she said, in a tone that did not sound very welcoming.

''ope I'm not intrudin', miss,' said Mr. Budd, apologetically. 'Thought as I was passin' I'd call in an' 'ave a word with you . . . '

'Come in,' she invited, rather unwillingly, and he followed her into the studio-sitting-room. 'I'm terribly busy,' she said. 'I've a book-jacket design which must be in the post this evening, so I'm afraid I shan't be able to talk for long . . . '

'That's all right, miss,' he answered, cheerfully. 'I'm pretty busy myself. I s'pose you've 'eard the news . . . '

'About Mrs. Brockwell?' she said, and nodded her head quickly. 'Yes. The whole village is full of it. You didn't come to see me about that, did you? You came because you've heard that my father was Mrs. Naylor's brother?'

Mr. Budd was a little taken aback. This was carrying the war into the enemy's camp with a vengeance.

'Well, partly, but not entirely, miss,' he answered. 'I came to 'ave a sort of general talk.'

'Very interesting,' said Harriet, coolly. 'What topic shall we begin with?'

'When did you last see Mr. Naylor?' asked the big man.

'Yesterday evening,' she answered, at once. 'He came here just after five and he left at half-past eight. Didn't the man who followed him tell you?'

So Naylor was aware that his movements were being watched, thought Mr. Budd. He said:

'Well, yes, he did.'

'Then why did you ask me?' demanded Harriet. She saw his discomfiture and laughed. 'You're wasting your time over Roger,' she said. '*He* didn't have anything to do with these murders. Neither did I.'

He looked at her steadily.

'No, I don't think either of you did,' he said, candidly. 'If I'd thought so you'd 'ave been arrested by now . . . '

'Then why are you having Roger watched?' she asked.

'More a matter of routine an' precaution than anythin' else,' he replied. 'Just in case I might be wrong . . . '

'You're a queer man for a detective,' she said, looking at him curiously. 'You know, I rather like you . . . '

'Thank you, miss,' murmured Mr. Budd.

'You don't *look* very clever,' she went on, thoughtfully. 'But I believe you are . . . '

'I 'aven't been very clever up ter now,' he said, with a rueful grimace. 'I didn't know you knew Tommy Custer, miss.'

'You saw him leave here just now, I

suppose?' she said, and he nodded. 'I thought perhaps you had,' she continued. 'Yes, I know him, though I don't expect you'd ever guess how I made his acquaintance. He's got a criminal record, hasn't he?'

'Did he tell you that?' asked Mr. Budd, in surprise.

'No, but I guessed he had,' she replied. 'You see, the circumstances in which I first met him were — well, peculiar. He broke into my father's studio in Kensington one night, and I surprised him. Of course, he told me a lovely story about having a wife and five children, and that this was the first time he'd ever done such a thing, and that if I would let him go, he'd go straight in future. I didn't believe a word of it, but I let him go because he was such an amusing little man . . . '

''e's also an expert burglar,' interposed Mr. Budd.

'Yes, I know,' she nodded. 'He told me all about it when father painted him. Oh, yes, he did, you know. He came down just as Tommy was saying 'good night and Gawd bless yer' to me and engaged him at once for a model. I should imagine it was the first honest piece of work that Tommy had ever done. The picture was exhibited and bought by Lord Shaterly. Father called it *The Thief*. Custer was immensely proud of it.'

Mr. Budd rubbed his fleshy chin and eyed her thoughtfully.

'So you know Tom Custer pretty well?' he remarked. 'It must have been a surprise to yer when he turned up in Long Millford as Brockwell's butler.'

'Well, as a matter of fact, it wasn't,' she said, calmly. 'I don't know whether I'm wise in telling you this, but I'm going to risk it. Anyway, there are no witnesses and if you tried to do anything about it, I should deny it. It was I who got Tommy that job.'

'Oh, it was, eh?' murmured Mr. Budd, raising his eyebrows. 'Now that's very interesting. Why did you do that?'

She helped herself to a cigarette from a box on the littered paint table and lit it.

'I wanted to get back on Brockwell for what he did to my father,' she replied, coolly, blowing out a cloud of blue smoke and watching it float up to the ceiling. 'I thought, with Tommy Custer installed in the house, I might get some of that three thousand pounds back that he tricked my father out of — or perhaps a bit more . . .'

'I see,' Mr. Budd pursed his lips. 'What was you thinkin' of goin' for?' he asked. 'Jewellery, or the fam'ly plate?'

'Neither,' she answered. 'Nothing so crude as *that*. I'll admit that *was* the first idea, but something happened to give me a better one. It was when Custer told me how the bills were paid. He brought his book every month to Brockwell with the tradesmen's accounts, and Brockwell wrote out a cheque for the *full* amount, so that each separate bill could be paid in cash. The cheque was made out to 'self' and Custer paid over the money and brought back the various receipts . . . Every now and again he went to the bank and drew out a larger sum — sometimes for two and three thousand pounds — and these cheques were always accompanied by a covering letter to the manager . . .'

Mr. Budd whistled softly.

'That's a lot o' money,' he said. 'What did he want all that money in cash for?'

She shrugged her shoulders.

'Mrs. Brockwell and the children were very extravagant,' she said, 'and they always paid for everything in cash. They seemed to have an objection to cheques . . . '

'How often were these large sums drawn out?' he asked.

'About once every six months,' she answered.

'H'm, an' I s'pose your idea was ter pinch the proceeds o' one of these cheques?' he remarked, but she shook her head.

'No, *my* idea was to alter one of the smaller cheques with chemicals and make it for a large amount, using the covering letter, with the date altered, to get it cashed without question.'

'But 'ow were you goin' ter get hold of the coverin' letter?' asked the interested detective. 'Surely the bank kept it . . . ?'

'Custer was going to present one of the *authentic* cheques *without* the covering letter,' she replied. 'We thought that the bank, after so long, would cash the cheque without question. If there was any fuss about it, all Custer had to say was that he had lost the letter . . . '

'You'd 'ave all been in gaol inside a month,' commented Mr. Budd.

'Perhaps we should, perhaps we shouldn't,' said Harriet Lake. 'We should have faked the trades-people's receipts to account for the proceeds of the altered cheque — the *original* amount, I mean. That would have given quite a long time for Custer to clear out and go abroad with his share. Nobody would have been able to connect *me* with the matter at all. However, as I said, it was my *idea*. I decided not to attempt to carry it out. That's why I'm telling you all about it . . . '

'I think you're very wise not to attempt it, either, miss,' said Mr. Budd. 'I 'ope that Tommy Custer ain't thinkin' o' tryin' on his own account?'

'He won't,' she said, 'although he was heart-broken when I told him I'd given up the idea. That was before the murder of John Brockwell. After *that* we'd have had to give it up in any case.'

Mr. Budd regarded her speculatively from under drooping lids. Had she given up the idea of stealing this money from Brockwell *before* the first murder? Or had that been cause and effect? It was impossible to tell. He felt that his first estimate of Harriet Lake had been right. She would tell you just as much as she wanted to tell you and no more. A queer girl, but rather nice.

'Well, miss,' he said, 'you've been very frank about it, I must say. Were you expectin' Custer that first day I come 'ere ter tea?'

She nodded.

'Yes, I was rather disappointed he didn't come. I should like to have seen both your faces.'

Mr. Budd laughed, a throaty, chuckling rumble that shook his large paunch.

'Instead o' which you got a bit of a shock yerself when Mr. Naylor turned up?' he said. 'You didn't, by any chance, give Custer a note to deliver to Brockwell, did yer?'

'No,' she said. Why?'

'It doesn't matter. I just wanted ter make sure it wasn't you,' he said. She looked at him curiously, but before she could frame the question on her lips, he continued: 'What puzzles me, miss, among a lot of other things, is why your father, knowin' 'ow Brockwell 'ad treated 'is brother-in-law, should 'ave allowed himself ter be swindled? I can't understand that . . . '

Harriet Lake stubbed out her cigarette in an ash-tray, and she wasn't looking at him when she replied:

'It does seem strange, doesn't it?'

'Very strange, miss,' said Mr. Budd. 'Can you account for it?'

'I think I could,' she said, looking up suddenly, 'but I don't think I'm going to . . . '

7

An attempt was made to murder Henry Brockwell that evening. He and Mr. Budd and Sergeant Leek had dinner together in the big dining-room. He was in his most taciturn mood and scarcely spoke at all throughout the meal, grunting now and again as his contribution towards the conversation.

Mr. Budd did not greatly mind this lack of oral entertainment on the part of his host. He had plenty to occupy his thoughts, and was content to eat his food in his usual slow manner, and ruminate. The melancholy Leek, who never talked very much, anyway, was relieved that he was not called upon to exercise his limited conversational powers. Brockwell drank a good deal during the meal, consuming nearly half a freshly opened bottle of Johnnie Walker, but it seemed to have little effect on him beyond heightening the normal redness of his face and inflaming his small, pig-like eyes.

Coffee was served in the drawing-room and Brockwell drained his cup at a gulp and poured himself out a generous portion of brandy from a partly full bottle that stood on a side-table. Raising the glass to his lips, he paused and sniffed.

''ullo,' he said, thickly, 'what's the matter with this? Queer sorta smell about it — like almonds . . . ' He thrust the glass towards Mr. Budd. 'What d'you think of it, eh?'

The big man took it and sniffed in his turn. There was a strong and distinct odour of almonds.

'I think you'd better leave it alone,' he said, sharply. 'It's my belief it's been poisoned.'

'Poisoned?' Brockwell blinked at him. ''ow the devil could it 'ave been . . . ?'

''ow long 'as that bottle been there?' asked Mr. Budd.

'It's always there — that or another,' answered Brockwell. 'I always keep a selection o' drinks on that table . . . '

Mr. Budd went over and inspected the contents of the table. There was a full bottle of whisky, a half-empty bottle of gin, a syphon of soda-water, and the partly used bottle of brandy. He picked up the gin, removed the cork and smelt it. There was no trace of the almond smell here. The whisky bottle was unopened and still retained its seal and he passed that by, turning his attention to the brandy. The smell of almonds greeted his nostrils strongly.

'Somethin's been put in the brandy,' he said. ''ydrocyanic acid, or somethin' like it. Go an' ring up Doctor Middlesham an' ask 'im ter pop up 'ere, will you, Leek? Do you always 'ave brandy after yer dinner?'

Brockwell, to whom the question had been addressed, nodded.

'When did yer last 'ave any from this bottle?' asked Mr. Budd. 'Last night, was it?'

'No, I didn't 'ave none last night,' said Brockwell. 'I 'ad whisky . . . '

'You was lucky,' answered the detective. 'You 'ad brandy the night before. I remember seein' yer . . . ' He pursed his lips and pulled irritably at his right ear.

311

'Whatever was put in that bottle was put there between then an' now,' he muttered.

'But who could 'ave put it there?' demanded Brockwell.

'There was somebody in the 'ouse yesterday,' said Mr. Budd. 'Somebody who 'id in the linen cupboard upstairs. I should say that was the person what put the poison in the brandy. If it *is* poison,' he added.

'I can't stand this!' Brockwell's voice shook in his agitation. 'I can't stand it! Yer've got ter do somethin' . . . '

'Everythin' that can be done is *bein'* done,' said Mr. Budd, with a conviction that he was far from feeling. The discovery of the poison in the brandy had shaken him. If Brockwell hadn't noticed that smell of almonds . . . He refused to contemplate the consequences.

'I've got ter get away,' muttered Brockwell, lighting a cigarette with shaking hands. 'I've *got* to. Don' you understand . . . ?'

'Now, take it easy,' said Mr. Budd, reassuringly.

'It's all very well fer *you*,' said

Brockwell. 'Nobody's tryin' ter kill *you* . . . '

'A good many people 'ave in me time,' said Mr. Budd. 'But I'm still alive an' kickin' . . . It's no good your talkin' about goin' away. It 'ud be the stupidest thing you could do. While you're 'ere we can see that you're well guarded . . . '

'Whoever it is must be a devil,' exclaimed Brockwell. 'You say 'e 'id in the linen cupboard? 'ow d'yer know . . . ?'

Mr. Budd explained.

'An' yer think it may be Edie's husband?' said Brockwell. 'I've tried ter remember what 'is name was, but I can't . . . '

'I've had a cable sent to Ontario,' said the big man. 'We'll know the name some time ter-morrow, I should think . . . '

'I've been thinkin' over your idea,' muttered Brockwell, 'an' there may be somethin' in it . . . The feller was class . . . 'e came from a classy fam'ly, but 'e 'adn't two pennies ter rub together . . . no ruddy good, either . . . '

''ave you got a lawyer?' asked Mr. Budd, suddenly struck with an idea.

'Yes. What . . . ?' began Brockwell, in surprise.

'Could you get 'old of him ter-morrer?' interrupted the big man, and Brockwell nodded. 'Get 'im,' said Mr. Budd. 'Get 'im ter come down 'ere . . . '

'What for?' demanded Brockwell. 'A lawyer ain't goin' ter 'elp . . . '

'Isn't 'e?' said Mr. Budd. 'Look 'ere. If this idea o' mine's right, your sister an' 'er 'usband come inter the money if anything happens to you. That's what we figure out's the motive behind this business. Well, you make another will leavin' yer money to someone else an' the motive's gone. Nobody's goin' to kill you for nothin' . . . '

Brockwell drew a sudden, quick breath.

'I should've thought of it before,' went on the stout superintendent.

'It won't do any good if you're not right,' said Brockwell.

'It can't do any 'arm, anyway,' said Mr. Budd.

'But 'ow is it goin' ter get out that I've made this 'ere will?' asked Brockwell. 'It's no good unless they 'ear about it . . . '

Leek came in before the big man could reply.

'I ain't 'alf 'ad a job findin' Middlesham,' he said, plaintively. 'I got 'im at last, though, at Sir Oswald Pipp-Partington's. 'e's coming along at once . . . '

'Good,' said Mr. Budd. 'We'll make sure that that stuff in the brandy *is poison*, though I 'aven't much doubt about it, meself . . . They ought ter 'ear about it if we spread it around the district. Don't forget the murderer must be in the district . . . '

'Well, I s'pose there's no 'arm in tryin' it,' grunted Brockwell. 'I'll get on ter my lawyer first thing in the mornin'.'

'Eh?' Mr. Budd had apparently not been listening and Brockwell had to repeat it. A point had suddenly occurred to him, and it was a very important point. Supposing that his theory regarding Brockwell's sister and her husband to be right, *how did they know that by eliminating the Brockwell family they would come into the money?* It was such an obvious point that he was annoyed with himself for not having thought of it before. It was scarcely likely that they would have planned, and carried out, a whole series of murders without making *certain* that they would reap the reward at the end. And how had they managed to *make* certain? Brockwell might have made fifty wills for all they knew, and it was *only* if he died *without a will* that they could hope to inherit as next of kin. Somehow or other they must have made *sure*.

The big man sighed involuntarily. Whenever you thought things were going easily in this business, you came up against a snag. And this was a pretty big snag. Maybe Brockwell himself could help? He explained the difficulty.

'I don' know 'ow they coulda known,' replied Brockwell, frowning. 'Unless they got it out o' John, or James, or Sandra. *They* knew . . . '

'Did they know this man your sister married?' asked Mr. Budd, and Brockwell shook his head.

'No, o' course they didn't,' he said, ungraciously. ''ow could they? They wouldn't be old enough . . . '

'I see,' said the big man, and he breathed more freely. Perhaps the snag wasn't so formidable after all. If John Brockwell had known that the only will in existence was the one in which his father left all his money equally divided between his wife and children, John could have passed on the information before he died . . . That was what had probably happened. And if he didn't know to whom he was giving the information, he wouldn't have realized its significance.

Doctor Middlesham arrived, in a violent hurry, but full of interest over the latest development.

'Never a dull moment,' he said to Mr. Budd, and gave Brockwell a brusque nod, making no effort to hide his dislike. 'Now, what's all this about poison?'

Mr. Budd told him, and gave him the glass of brandy.

Middlesham sniffed at it, made a wry face, and set it down carefully.

'Characteristic smell of hydrocyanic acid,' he said. 'But it could quite as easily be almond essence. Can't tell until it's properly tested. I'll take it along to my

317

surgery and let you know.'

'Thank you, doctor,' said Mr. Budd. 'Whatever it is, it's in the bottle, too. No, don't touch it, please. There may be prints . . .'

'All right,' said Middlesham. 'Got anything I can take the contents of the glass in?'

'Ring for Custer,' grunted Brockwell, curtly, and Leek did so.

The little man came, uneasily curious.

'What's goin' on?' he demanded.

'Mind yer own business!' snarled Brockwell.

'I want a small bottle, large enough to take the contents of this glass,' said Middlesham. 'And it must be quite clean. Can you manage that?'

Mr. Custer said he thought he could and went away to try.

'That feller's gettin' above 'imself,' growled Brockwell. 'I'm goin' ter send 'im packin'.'

'How did this poison, supposing it *is* poison, get in the bottle of brandy?' asked Doctor Middlesham, ignoring Brockwell's remark completely.

Mr. Budd shook his head.

'It's a matter o' speculation,' he answered, slowly. 'There was somebody who shouldn't 'ave been in the house, 'iding in a linen cupboard yesterday. We think that's 'ow it was done, but we ain't sure.'

Middlesham formed his lips into a silent whistle.

'Whoever is at the bottom of all this, seems to be pretty determined,' he said. 'They don't believe in wasting time, apparently.'

Brockwell gave him a venomous glare.

'If I 'adn't noticed the smell an' drunk that stuff, I might have been dead by now,' he said.

'If it's hydrocyanic acid you probably would be,' agreed Middlesham, cheerfully. 'It's very pungent stuff. Acts in two or three seconds . . . '

'An' it ain't easy ter get hold of,' remarked Mr. Budd. 'You can't just walk into a shop an' buy it.'

'Very difficult indeed,' said Middlesham. 'You've probably got something there. You should be able to trace where it came from . . . '

319

'I'd thought o' that,' said Mr. Budd. 'Unless, o' course, this person we're after turns out ter be a chemist or a doctor . . . '

'Or a vet,' said Middlesham. 'Yes, they could all three get hold of it fairly easily . . . '

''ave you got any in your surgery, doctor?' asked Mr. Budd.

'No,' said Middlesham. 'No occasion to use it . . . '

A knock at the door heralded the return of Mr. Custer. He brought with him a small, two-ounce bottle.

'Will this do yer?' he asked.

'The very thing.' Middlesham took it, held it up to the light, and finally removed the cork and sniffed. 'Seems clean enough, too,' he said. With great care he poured the contents of the brandy glass into the bottle, corked it carefully, and slipped it into his pocket, while Tommy Custer looked on, obviously bursting with curiosity.

'Well, I must be off,' said Middlesham. 'Clarissa's waiting for me in the car. I'll phone through the result of the test later.'

He went swiftly over to the door with long strides. 'By the way,' he said, stopping on the threshold. 'You'd better let me have some of the brandy out of the bottle when you're through with it. We'll have to check up on that as well, you know.'

'I'll send it along to yer,' said Mr. Budd, and Middlesham nodded and was gone.

'Can yer get me a piece o' brown paper?' asked Mr. Budd, and when it was brought to him, wrapped up the bottle of brandy, left the unenthusiastic Leek to look after Brockwell and, getting out his ancient car, drove over to Bedlington.

Superintendent Tidworthy was just going home when he reached the police station, but the news which the big man brought interested him so much that he stayed while the tests were made. The result was negative. The only prints on the bottle were Brockwell's.

'The person who put the stuff in was careful an' wore gloves,' said Mr. Budd. 'Well, I can't say I expected anythin' else . . .'

Tidworthy stroked the top of his bald head and looked very serious.

'The next time they may get away with it,' he said, gloomily. 'You can't test everything the man's going to eat or drink . . . '

'I know,' agreed Mr. Budd, 'but they won't 'ave such an opportunity again. I'm 'avin' the house searched thoroughly every night an' mornin'.'

'Well, I hope they don't,' said Tidworthy, without a great deal of optimism.

'There's one thing I'd like yer ter do,' said Mr. Budd, as he got into his car. 'Find out who bought any hydrocyanic acid, or prussic acid, in the district within the last eighteen months. 'ave the inquiry made over as wide an area as possible. It might give us something . . . '

Mr. Custer was waiting in the hall when he got back.

'That doctor feller 'phoned up about twenty minutes ago,' he said. 'Bit annoyed 'e seemed ter find you wasn't in . . . '

'Did he leave any message?' asked Mr. Budd.

'No,' answered the little man. ''e said

'e'd ring up again . . . '

The telephone bell trilled insistently, breaking into the end of his sentence.

'I'll bet that's 'im now,' declared Mr. Custer.

It *was* Middlesham.

'I've tested that brandy,' he said. 'It's so chock full of hydrocyanic acid that a sip would kill a regiment.'

'Thanks, doctor,' said Mr. Budd. 'You'd better 'ang on ter what's left. It'll 'ave to go up to the analyst . . . '

'Right you are,' said Middlesham. 'Any prints on the bottle?'

'Only Brockwell's,' answered Mr. Budd, and rang off.

'Wot's bin 'appening?' asked Tom Custer, at his elbow. 'Somebody bin tryin' ter bump off 'is nibs?'

'What makes yer think that?' said the big man, yawning.

'I was listenin' at the door,' replied Custer, quite unabashed at the admission. 'Cor blimey, ter think I might 'ave 'ad a nip outta that bottle meself . . . '

'Let it be a warnin' ter yer not to go about nippin' things,' said Mr. Budd, severely. 'I saw yer friend, Miss 'arriet Lake, to-day . . . '

'My friend?' Mr. Custer gaped at him. 'I dunno . . . '

'It's no good, Tommy. She told me all about it,' interrupted Mr. Budd, and the consternation on the little man's face was almost ludicrous.

'She . . . Cor blimey, yer can't never trust a woman, can yer?' said Tommy Custer, bitterly. 'Why couldn't she keep 'er mouth shut . . . ?'

'There's no 'arm done, so yer needn't worry,' said Mr. Budd. 'Now come along. We're goin' to search the 'ouse, an' make sure we ain't got no unexpected visitors, before you lock up for the night.'

By the time they had done this and made sure there was nobody hiding in any of the rooms, or cupboards, Mr. Budd was almost dropping with fatigue. The exertions of the day, added to his almost sleepless night, had worn him out. He made sure that Leek was at his post beside Brockwell and then he went to bed. His head had barely touched the pillow before he was fast asleep . . .

8

The morning was fine and hot and it looked as though another spell of good weather had set in. Mr. Budd woke early and felt better for a long and dreamless sleep. He drank his morning tea, had a bath, shaved, dressed and went to have a look at Leek and Brockwell. The lean sergeant was dozing, and Brockwell was asleep, or pretending to be. The big man left them and went downstairs. While he waited for his breakfast, he took a stroll in the sunshine outside. The rest, and the change in the weather, had made him feel less pessimistic. There was little else to account for his sudden change of mood.

Just as he was finishing his breakfast, Tommy Custer announced an unexpected visitor. Mr. Joshua Craven came into the room with his usual sedate manner, but with a trace of diffidence about him that was not so usual.

'Good morning,' he said. 'I hope that

you will forgive this early call. I was afraid that if I left it later you might be out . . . '

'What d'you want?' grunted Mr. Budd.

'May I sit down?' Without waiting for an answer, Mr. Craven perched himself on a chair. He looked, thought Mr. Budd, rather like an undertaker who had called to make arrangements for a funeral. 'How are you — er — progressing with the case?'

'Did you come 'ere to try an' pump me?' demanded Mr. Budd, bluntly, and the reporter looked shocked.

'Dear me, no,' he replied, shaking his head. 'I doubt very much whether you could — er — supply me with any — er — valuable information. I fear — quite without offence, you understand — that you have failed to grasp the essential point in this affair . . . '

'Have *you*?' demanded Mr. Budd.

'Well, I rather think that I have,' said Mr. Craven, with the ghost of a complacent smile.

'What is it?'

'Oh, come, come now,' protested the reporter. 'You surely don't imagine that I am going to tell you, my dear sir. I have my living to get, remember . . . '

'Withholdin' information that may be important to a p'lice investigation,' said Mr. Budd, 'is a serious matter.'

'I know all the rules,' replied Joshua Craven, unimpressed. 'There's nothing that enforces me to divulge a theory . . . '

'Oh, is that all it is?' The big man sniffed, disparagingly. 'It's easy enough ter form theories.'

'But not always so easy to form the right ones,' remarked the reporter. 'The Pipp-Partingtons are very charming people, don't you think?'

'I've only met 'em once,' said Mr. Budd, wondering at the reason for this sudden, sharp tangent in the conversation. 'Can't say I know much about 'em.'

'A very old family,' went on Mr. Craven. 'Very old indeed. The line goes back for centuries. It's curious how the cadet members of these ancient families sometimes go off the rails. Very curious and very sad, too.' He shook his head sorrowfully. 'It must have been a great tragedy for Sir Oswald Pipp-Partington when his son turned out to be a black sheep . . . '

'His son?' echoed Mr. Budd. 'I knew he had a daughter, but I didn't know he 'ad a son . . . '

'A charming girl,' said Mr. Craven, enthusiastically. 'A type that can, with reason, be called an English beauty . . . Oh, yes, he has a son, though I believe he is never mentioned now, and has been disinherited. Of course, he's much older than Miss Clarissa — he must be twenty years older — yes, quite that. He did something discreditable when he was a young man and had to go abroad. I believe the police were after him and he changed his name to Travis. Sir Oswald and Lady Pipp-Partington were, naturally, very upset, but I suppose after all this time they've got over it. Time is a wonderful healer, a wonderful anodyne . . . ' Mr. Craven coughed gently. 'Do you think I might be permitted to see Mr. Brockwell for a few moments?'

He had a habit of suddenly going off on a fresh topic, which was very disconcerting.

'What d'you want to see *him* for?' asked Mr. Budd.

'Just so that I can get my angles right,' answered Mr. Craven. 'I have never met him, and I should like to include an interview with him in the article I am writing for *The Globe News* . . . '

'You can see 'im if he'll let you,' grunted Mr. Budd. '*I*'ve no objection.'

'Thank you, that's extremely good of you,' said Mr. Craven, with a great display of gratitude. 'Can I send my card to him?'

Mr. Budd rang for Custer, and the little man was dispatched, with the card, to his master. He returned while Mr. Craven was eulogizing on the beauties of the English countryside.

''e says you can go ter 'ell!' said Tommy Custer, bluntly.

'A trifle crude, but understandable,' said the reporter. He rose to his feet. 'Well, perhaps there are other methods of approach . . . I needn't keep you any longer, I'm sure you have plenty to do. A difficult case, my dear sir, a *very* difficult case.'

He departed, shaking his head sadly

over the difficulty of the case, and left Mr. Budd to ponder on his visit.

He was still pondering when the telephone rang and Mr. Custer thrust in his head to say briefly:

'Scotland Yard wants yer.'

Mr. Budd lumbered heavily out to the instrument.

''ello?' he called.

'Is that Superintendent Budd?' said the telephone. 'Inspector Pike here, sir. We've just received an answer to the cable you asked us to send to Ontario. I thought perhaps you'd like to have it read to you over the phone to save time in case the matter was urgent . . . '

'Go ahead,' said Mr. Budd.

''*Re* your inquiry 10/18076/19. Message begins. Edith Brockwell, spinster, was married to Everard Travis on November 18th, 19 — , at Central Registry Office, Ontario. Message ends.''

'Everard *Travis*, did you say?' exclaimed Mr. Budd, incredulously.

'That's right, sir. T.R.A.V.I.S.,' said the telephone. 'I'll forward the original cable at once, sir. Is there anything else?'

'No . . . no, thank yer, Pike,' murmured Mr. Budd, abruptly, and he hung up the receiver.

Everard Travis . . . Henry Brockwell's sister had married Everard Travis. And Everard Travis, according to Mr. Craven, was Everard Pipp-Partington, the only son of Sir Oswald and Lady Pipp-Partington . . .

Mr. Budd walked slowly back to the dining-room. This was the man who, if his theory was correct, was responsible for the murders. And he was somewhere close at hand . . . All he had to do now was to find him; and that, he decided ruefully, was not going to be the easiest thing in the world.

Part Five

The Ace of Diamonds

1

'Of course,' said Major Toppington, staring at the end of his cigar, 'I knew there *was* a son. Most people knew that. But I'd no idea that he had married, or whom. There was an unholy scandal at the time he was chucked out. I was only a young man then, but I remember it very well . . . '

'What did 'e do, sir?' asked Mr. Budd. He had driven over to Bedlington and sought out the Chief Constable almost immediately after receiving the telephone call from Scotland Yard.

'He got mixed up in a very unsavoury business indeed,' said Toppington. He spoke reluctantly, as though he had little relish in resuscitating this long-buried scandal. 'He stole a necklace at a house-party. He'd got into serious debt and he was desperate. It broke up Sir Oswald. He'd been very proud of his son, but when he heard what he'd done, he

335

was adamant. He refused to have anything more to do with him at all. Everard finally forged a cheque for two hundred pounds and fled to Canada. The police tried to trace him, but they failed, because, I suppose, he'd changed his name to Travis . . . '

'An' 'avin' changed it once, he's probably changed it again,' murmured Mr. Budd. 'I don't think there's much doubt that my idea was right, sir.'

'I'm sorry to have to admit it,' said the Chief Constable, 'but I don't think there is, either. I should say that Everard Pipp-Partington, to give him his real name, would be quite capable of whole-sale murder, if he was going to make enough out of it.'

'Well, our job now, sir,' said Mr. Budd, 'is to find him. He can't be very far away, but it's goin' ter be a bit like lookin' for a pebble on Brighton beach . . . '

Major Toppington nodded.

'Yes, not too easy,' he agreed. 'I expect he's changed a pretty good bit in twenty years and, anyway, he wouldn't risk coming to this district without taking care to alter his appearance so that there'd be no danger of recognition. Yes, we're going to have all our work cut out to find him. However, at last we know who we're looking for, and that's something. It was a good job of work on your part, Superintendent.'

'Thank you, sir,' murmured Mr. Budd. 'Our best way of catchin' 'im, I think, sir, would be to set a trap . . . '

'How do you mean?' broke in the Chief Constable.

'Well,' explained the big man, ''e's got ter *finish* the job. There's no money in it until 'e's killed Brockwell, you see. An' 'aving gone so far, he's not likely to give up at the last lap, so to speak. When he learns that the poison in the brandy didn't do the trick, 'e'll try again. Now if we could sort o' make it easy for 'im, sir . . . '

'I see what you're driving at,' said Major Toppington, gravely, 'but you'd be taking a colossal risk. Supposing he succeeded . . . '

'We'd 'ave to ensure that 'e couldn't,' said Mr. Budd, quickly. 'At the present moment we're guardin' Brockwell openly.

He's never left night or day, an' it 'ud be practically impossible fer anyone ter get at him, except by poison, and even *that* wouldn't be so easy. But s'pose we relax all our precautions an' leave 'im apparently vulnerable. This feller'll seize his opportunity, an' we can grab 'im.'

Major Toppington carefully deposited a cylinder of cigar ash in an ash-tray at his elbow.

'Well,' he remarked, after a thoughtful pause, 'it would have to be very carefully carried out . . .'

They discussed the matter further at great length and decided on a plan.

'I should be glad, sir,' said Mr. Budd, just before he left, 'if you could arrange for Sup'n'tendent Tidworthy ter take my place at Brockwell's. I want ter go up to London . . .'

He reached Scotland Yard in the early afternoon, and at once sought an interview with the Assistant Commissioner. Colonel Blair was inclined to be a little frosty at first, but he thawed quite a good deal when he heard what the big man had to say.

338

'Well, you appear to have redeemed yourself, Budd,' he said, 'even if it is at the eleventh hour. Of course, you've still got to find this man, but you seem to have worked it out very neatly. You can have all the assistance you want . . . '

Mr. Budd left the office with his object achieved. He went in search of Inspector Pike.

'I want yer ter try an' trace that feller Travis who married Edith Brockwell,' he said. ''is real name is Everard Pipp-Partington. I want ter know his movements from the time of 'is marriage up ter date. Can yer do that?'

'It's a tall order,' answered Pike, cheerfully, 'but we'll do our best, sir. By the way, here's the report on the past history of Brockwell which you asked for. It's just been completed. There are several gaps, I'm afraid, but it's the best we could do.'

He produced a thin wad of typescript and handed it to Mr. Budd.

'I'll look at it when I get back,' said the stout superintendent, folding it and stowing it away in his breast pocket. 'Now, yer'll get on ter that right away, won't yer?

I want that information as quick as you can possibly get it.'

Inspector Pike promised that he would do his best, and Mr. Budd, after a brief visit to his own cheerless office, left the Yard and drove to his small house in Streatham. Here he stayed long enough to inspect his beloved roses, and pick up some clean shirts and underclothing, and then set off on his return trip to Long Millford. It was dusk when he reached the village and he drove straight to Sir Oswald Pipp-Partington's.

The old butler, Flower, opened the door in answer to his knock and looked a little surprised to see him.

'Sir Oswald is just finishing dinner, sir,' he said, in reply to Mr. Budd's inquiry. 'I'll inform him that you wish to see him . . .'

'I don't mind waitin',' said the big man. 'Please tell 'im that the matter is rather urgent or I wouldn't 'ave bothered 'im . . .'

The butler inclined his head and went away to deliver the message. In a few minutes he was back.

'Sir Oswald says if you will wait for fifteen minutes he will see you,' he said. 'Please come this way.'

He conducted Mr. Budd to the room in which he had waited before, and left him. At the expiration of exactly fifteen minutes he returned.

'Sir Oswald will see you now, sir,' he said. Mr. Budd followed him to the library, and Sir Oswald Pipp-Partington greeted him courteously.

'I am sorry to have kept you waiting, Superintendent,' he said.

'I'm afraid I called at a bit of an awkward time, sir,' said Mr. Budd. 'I 'ope I 'aven't inconvenienced you too . . . '

'No, no,' interrupted Sir Oswald. 'Would you like a glass of port? I can thoroughly recommend it. Alas, I fear, there are not very many bottles left now.' He touched a cut-glass decanter. 'This wine was laid down when my father was a boy at school,' he said. 'Flower — another glass . . . '

The butler fetched one, reverently filled it, and handed it to the detective on a silver tray.

'Thank you,' said Mr. Budd. He took a sip and savoured the smooth, velvety old wine. 'It's very good indeed, sir,' he said.

'I was sure that you would like it,' replied Sir Oswald. 'And now, what can I do for you?'

Mr. Budd hesitated. He realized that this interview was going to be difficult for him and painful for the grey-haired man who was regarding him so steadily.

'Well, sir,' he said, slowly, 'I'm afraid that what I've come about may not be very pleasant for you. Unfortunately, 'owever, it's my duty an' I've got ter do it . . .'

Sir Oswald frowned — a slightly perplexed frown.

'I don't think I understand,' he said. 'What is there that I should find — er — unpleasant . . . ?'

Mr. Budd took another sip of port.

'It's about your son, sir,' he said, bluntly.

The lined face of the man before him seemed to grow more aged. His mouth puckered and his eyes clouded.

'I have no son,' he answered, harshly.

'I know about the trouble,' said Mr. Budd, uncomfortably. 'I'm very sorry, sir, that I've got ter rake all this up . . . '

'Why have you got to?' asked Sir Oswald. 'What have my private family affairs to do with you?'

'Your son, sir — Mr. Everard Pipp-Partington — married Miss Edith Brockwell in Ontario eighteen years ago. Miss Brockwell is Mr. 'enry Brockwell's sister . . . '

'*What?*' Sir Oswald reached out a thin hand and gripped the back of a chair. The bony knuckles stood out milk-white with the force of his grip. 'What's that you say . . . ?'

''e was married in the name of Everard Travis,' said Mr. Budd. 'You didn't know this, sir?'

Sir Oswald shook his grey head.

'No,' he answered, and the big man saw that he was making a desperate effort to retain his composure. 'No . . . I have neither heard, nor seen, anything of . . . my son . . . since . . . since . . . '

''e went away,' murmured Mr. Budd, gently. 'I understand, sir. I 'ope you'll try ter be equally understandin', sir, when

343

you 'ear what I'm goin' ter say. I don't like 'avin' ter say it, but . . . '

'Go on,' interrupted Sir Oswald. 'I fully realize your position . . . '

'Thank you, sir,' said Mr. Budd, gratefully. 'Well, you see, sir, your son marryin' 'enry Brockwell's sister like he did, makes 'er the next o' kin ter Brockwell's money . . . '

'I don't . . . quite understand,' said Sir Oswald. 'Could you be a little more explicit?' He had gained complete control of his emotions, but his face was a stony mask. Only the narrowed eyes showed any trace of the pain he was suffering.

'Well, sir,' said Mr. Budd. 'It's like this . . . ' As tactfully as was possible, he explained his theory. He couldn't cover up the actual accusation he was making against Everard Pipp-Partington, but he softened it as much as he was able.

'So you believe that my . . . son may be responsible for these murders?' said the old man. 'I'll not attempt to offer an opinion. You may be right, you may be wrong. What do you want of *me*?'

'I thought, before I came 'ere, sir,' answered Mr. Budd, 'that you might 'ave been able to give me some information concernin' the present whereabouts of your son . . . '

'And you think, if I had that information, I would divulge it?' asked Sir Oswald.

'Yes, sir,' said Mr. Budd, 'I think you would.'

'You pay a high tribute to my sense of duty, if not to my parental instincts, Superintendent,' said Sir Oswald. 'I wonder which would come uppermost if it were put to the test? Fortunately, or unfortunately, it cannot be put to the test. I know nothing whatever about my . . . son's whereabouts. For all I know he may be as dead, in reality, as he has been to me for all these years . . . '

Mr. Budd was convinced that he spoke the truth. He left him, a little deeper lined, and looking older than when he had come, but bearing his burden with all the proud stoicism of his breed.

2

When he got back to The Croft, Mr. Budd was a very weary man indeed. Sergeant Leek had gone to bed, and Mackleberry was on guard over Brockwell, who was sitting morosely in the drawing-room drinking whisky. Superintendent Tidworthy, he learned, had just gone, after leaving a message that the inquest on Mrs. Brockwell had been fixed for ten o'clock the following morning. There was nothing else to report. The day, during his absence, had been uneventful. Henry Brockwell said that he had telephoned to his lawyer, but he was unable to come down because he had to be in court all day. He gave the information in an off-hand, surly tone, and appeared to be thoroughly bad-tempered.

Mr. Budd had a meal in the dining-room. Brockwell had already dined, but Mr. Custer rose manfully to the occasion and produced some cold beef and salad, and a portion of apple pie. The big man ate heartily, for he had had nothing but a hasty sandwich since breakfast that morning.

It was Mackleberry's turn for duty until two o'clock, after which Leek would take over until the morning; and Mr. Budd decided, when he had finished his supper, to call it a day and go to bed.

While he was undressing, he recollected the type-written report which Pike had given him concerning Brockwell's past history. Taking it out of his breast pocket, he put it on the bedside table. It would, he thought, be a good idea to glance through it before he went to sleep.

Getting into bed, he settled himself comfortably, picked up the manuscript, and began to read . . .

It was nearly three hours later when he switched off the light and lay staring, wide awake, into the darkness. One brilliant, illuminating paragraph in that carefully compiled report had told him all that he wanted to know . . .

3

The inquest on the fourth victim of the unknown murderer created such a storm of interest that people came from all over the district in the hope of witnessing something sensational. Long before the proceedings started, the High Street at Long Millford was crowded with people and cars. The newspaper men were well to the fore with the exception of Mr. Joshua Craven, who was nowhere to be seen, and who, in fact, had gone up to London on the previous night and was at that particular moment engaged in searching the files of the *San Francisco Sun* with a great deal of patient diligence.

The Coroner was bad-tempered and inclined to be caustic. Superintendent Tidworthy told Mr. Budd, before the inquest opened, that he had had a great deal of trouble with the Coroner, who was strongly opposed to an adjournment and wished to undertake a full inquiry. It had only been on the personal intervention of Major Toppington that he had eventually, grudgingly, capitulated. His antagonism was obvious from the beginning. In his opening speech to the jury he alluded to the three previous crimes and made a sarcastic reference to the police investigation, and this attitude he adopted throughout the short proceedings. Mr. Budd, in particular, became a target for the Coroner's bitter disapproval, but he suffered the shafts of mordant witticisms with a stolid face of stoical indifference.

The request for an adjournment was reluctantly granted, and the inquiry came to an end.

'Have you begun the plan we discussed?' asked the Chief Constable, as they left the hall by a back exit to avoid the crowd.

Mr. Budd shook his head.

'No, sir,' he answered, slowly. 'I don't think it'll be necessary.'

'D'you mean that you've a better idea for finding Travis?' asked Major Toppington, in surprise.

'Well, not exactly,' said Mr. Budd. 'I don't think we shall have to find him now, sir . . .'

Major Toppington frowned and gave him a quick look.

'Then what *do* you mean?' he demanded, with some asperity.

Mr. Budd looked cautiously round to assure himself that he could not be overheard.

'I'll tell yer, sir,' he said, and proceeded to do so to the gathering amazement of his companion.

'Are you *sure*?' asked the Chief Constable, when he had finished.

'I think so, sir,' replied Mr. Budd. 'I don't think there's any doubt . . . '

'Good heavens,' muttered Major Toppington. 'It's incredible . . . under our noses all the time . . . '

'Those are the things yer don't usually see, sir,' said Mr. Budd.

★   ★   ★

The rest of the day passed slowly. Mr. Budd wandered restlessly about The Croft, apparently only half awake. Sergeant Leek, who knew from long experience what these outward signs portended, decided that there would very shortly be a period of intense activity, and sighed at the prospect. Mr. Custer went about his duties in his usual rather furtive manner, and privately longed for the time when he would be able to leave Long Millford and seek the delights and amenities of the Walworth Road. Mrs. Bleecher once more began to think, and talk, about leaving The Croft, and received a reassuring word from Mr. Budd that she would be able to do so before very long. The end of this complicated and worrying business was in sight, but the big man realized that it had to be handled very delicately. Even now that he knew the truth, the slightest false move would spoil everything. He felt like a man walking on eggshells . . .

Henry Brockwell grew more and more morose and nervous, and drank heavily. He made no secret of the fact that he was impatient to get away. It was his intention, he said, to go abroad as soon as permission was granted for him to leave The Croft. He hated the place and was going to put it up for sale, lock, stock, and barrel. It was obvious that he resented being forced to remain in Long Millford. He made no further mention of his solicitor coming down, and Mr. Budd did not trouble to reopen the subject because, now, it was unnecessary.

The stout superintendent felt that he would be very glad when the whole unsavoury business was over and he could leave this unwholesome atmosphere for good. The brief glimpse which he had had of his garden and his neat little villa had engendered a nostalgia that was growing rapidly with every passing hour. Well, with any luck, it shouldn't be long now . . .

Before dinner that night he had a whispered conference with Leek, and what he said brought a look of astonishment to the sergeant's lean face that was almost ludicrous.

'Yer don't mean,' he gasped, 'that . . . ?'

'Don't go openin' that big mouth of yours too wide,' said Mr. Budd, warningly. 'I shouldn't have said what I 'ave if I didn't mean it. Now you get along an' do what I tell yer . . . '

Henry Brockwell and the big man dined alone. Brockwell noted the absence of the melancholy sergeant and asked where he was.

''Avin' a sleep,' answered Mr. Budd. 'The amount o' sleep that feller can get through is amazin'.' Which was a gross slander, because at that moment Leek was being very busy indeed.

Brockwell was within measurable distance of being drunk when they went into the drawing-room for coffee, and Mr. Budd came to the conclusion that if he wanted to get coherent answers, or even any answers at all, to the questions he wished to ask him, it would be wise not to delay too long. In consequence he began as soon as Tommy Custer had shut the door behind him after pouring out the coffee.

''ave you ever 'eard of a man called Mays?' he asked, abruptly.

Brockwell, who was pouring himself out a stiff brandy from a new bottle of Hennessy's Three Star, started so violently that he nearly dropped the glass.

'Mays?' he repeated, thickly.

'Joe Mays,' said Mr. Budd. ''e ran a kind o' speakeasy an' gambling joint in

353

San Francisco about twenty years ago. He's dead now. 'e died about fifteen years ago. Somebody shot 'im in his office one night . . . '

'What's all this got ter do with me?' broke in Brockwell, harshly.

''e was a clever feller, Joe Mays,' continued Mr. Budd, without taking any notice of the interruption. 'One way an' another 'e made a lot o' money before 'e was bumped off — nearly three hundred thousand pounds in English money — an' it all went to 'is widow . . . '

Brockwell took a gulp of brandy.

'She was a girl what 'ad worked for 'im in the show 'e put on at this joint I was tellin' yer about,' went on Mr. Budd, 'an' 'e married 'er. 'er name, before she was married, was Helen Conyers. She changed it ter Mays, an' when Joe died she changed it again, within six months, ter Brockwell . . . '

'What's the idea of tellin' me all this?' demanded Brockwell, unsteadily.

'Because yer didn't seem ter know the name o' Mays when I mentioned it,' said Mr. Budd, blandly. 'I was just tryin' to remind yer who 'e was . . . '

'I don't need remindin',' snapped Brockwell. 'I don't want ter be reminded . . . '

'I'm surprised at that,' remarked the fat detective, 'because this feller did you a good turn by dyin' when he did . . . '

'Did me a good turn?' Brockwell swallowed the rest of his brandy and put down the glass with a bang.

'If by someone dyin' it enabled *me* ter marry a woman with three 'undred thousand quid, I should call it a good turn,' said Mr. Budd.

'It didn't do me much good,' grunted Brockwell. ''elen was as mean as the devil . . . '

'But you 'ad all this . . . ' Mr. Budd waved a hand around him. 'You was able ter live in luxury . . . '

Brockwell laughed. It was a strained, hysterical laugh. The brandy, which he had swallowed so quickly on the top of all the whisky he had drunk that day, was taking effect. He swayed slightly on his feet.

'Luxury?' he said, bitterly. 'Luxury . . . ? Livin' in a blasted gilded prison, that's what it was . . . ' He slurred the words.

355

'This ain't *my* idea o' comfort. It was what 'elen wanted, an' what she wanted she 'ad . . . She paid the piper an' called the ruddy tune . . . '

'So that will you told me about — the will you're s'posed to 'ave made leavin' all yer money divided between yer wife an' children, don't exist, an' never *did* exist,' said Mr. Budd, sternly. 'Because you didn't 'ave any money to leave 'em. It was your wife's . . . '

Brockwell peered at him with narrowed, bloodshot eyes.

'What are yer tryin' to get at?' he muttered, thickly. 'What are you tryin' ter get at . . . ?'

'I'm gettin' at this,' said Mr. Budd. 'You can tell me if I'm wrong. This two 'undred an' fifty thousand pounds, which was s'posed ter be yours, was your wife's. If 'er children — the children of Joe Mays, by the way, an' not yours — 'adn't been killed before 'er, the money would 'ave gone to them, or the eldest of 'em. An' now they're *all* killed, unless there's a will to the contrary, it goes to *you*?' He waited for Brockwell to confirm this statement, but the man only stared at him. 'Ain't that right?' he persisted.

'Yes . . . yes, tha's right,' said Brockwell, hoarsely.

'Why didn't yer say so before?' demanded Mr. Budd. 'Why did you say it was *your* money?'

Brockwell licked his dry lips. His red face was queerly mottled.

'I dunno . . . I didn't want people ter think it was 'er money,' he muttered, 'that I was livin' on 'er money . . . '

'Are you sure that *was* the reason?' said Mr. Budd. 'Are you sure it wasn't because the fact that it was yer wife's money gave *you* a pretty strong motive . . . '

'No!' broke in Brockwell, violently. 'No! What are yer tryin' to 'ang on me?'

'I'm goin' ter hang nuthin' on you but the truth,' said Mr. Budd. 'An' that's the truth, ain't it, Brockwell? *You* killed John, and Sandra, and James, an' finally your wife, just so as you could get that two 'undred an' fifty thousand pounds . . . '

'No!' screamed Brockwell, and the blood came surging back into his face until it was a fiery crimson with the veins standing out on his temples. 'No! It was Naylor, or Travis, or someone who killed 'em. Not me. 'ow could I 'ave killed 'elen? I was in me own room. 'ow could I 'ave done it . . . ?'

'You was in yer own room when we 'eard an explosion which we *thought* was the shot that killed 'er,' said Mr. Budd, 'but you actually killed 'er just after you took in that cocoa . . . '

'It's lies!' shouted Brockwell. 'Blasted, ruddy lies . . . '

'You quarrelled with 'er so that the sound of yer raised voices 'ud drown the 'pop' of the silenced pistol,' went on Mr. Budd, remorselessly, ignoring the outburst, 'an' then you smashed the cocoa cup an' poured cocoa from the jug over yerself an' then smashed that, shoutin' all the time as though you were still carryin' on the quarrel, although yer wife was dead by then. An' then yer dropped the card — the King o' Diamonds — an' arranged somethin' that 'ud explode later, an' make us think that *that* was the shot . . . '

'Lies!' cried Brockwell, livid with fury

and fear. 'Lies — all lies. You've failed an' you're tryin' to put this on ter me ter save yer face . . . '

'You've been a queer mixture o' cunnin', cleverness, an' stupidity,' said Mr. Budd, calmly, though his face was dewed with perspiration. 'An' you nearly got away with it — right up ter the last moment yer nearly got away with it . . . '

'You can't prove nuthin',' shouted Brockwell. 'It's only what yer think. You ain't got no evidence . . . '

There was a tap on the door and he swung round with his lips curled back in a snarl as Leek shambled into the room.

'Did you find it?' asked Mr. Budd, quickly, and he breathed a sigh of relief when the lean sergeant nodded.

'Yes,' he answered. 'It was 'idden away in a drawer in 'is room, under a lot o' shirts an' underclothes . . . ' He held out, wrapped in a handkerchief, a small revolver with an oblong cylinder of metal attached to the stubby barrel. Mr. Budd took it carefully, making sure that his fingers only came in contact with the handkerchief.

'*There*'s my evidence, Brockwell,' he said, 'an' it's goin' ter 'ang you . . . '

Brockwell opened his mouth, gave a queer gasp, and suddenly collapsed in a heap on the floor . . .

4

'I was never more thankful in me life,' declared Mr. Budd to Major Toppington two hours later, 'than when Leek came inter the room with that gun. I was puttin' up a bluff an', although I knew I was right, I couldn't 'ave proved a thing . . . '

'It's doubtful whether we shall have to prove anything in a court of law,' remarked the Chief Constable. 'Brockwell may never recover. Doctor Middlesham says there's a clot of blood on the brain . . . '

'Maybe it'll be best if 'e don't,' said the big man. 'The evidence we've got ain't too strong, an' a good counsel would make 'ay of it. Though he'd 'ave a job explainin' away that gun with the silencer an' only Brockwell's prints on it . . . '

'That and the motive,' said Major Toppington. 'Oh, yes, I think we shall have a fairly good case. How did you manage to work out how Brockwell had killed his wife?'

'Well, sir,' explained Mr. Budd, 'once I knew from that report that the money was Mrs. Brockwell's, which supplied Brockwell with a motive, it wasn't so difficult. 'e was the last person ter go inter 'er room, an' she 'adn't been seen or 'eard alive after he came out. The only thing that put us off was the explosion which we took to be the shot which killed 'er — that an' the driftin' smoke an' smell of burnt powder which was still in the room when I opened the door. But if this explosion 'ad bin *faked* by usin' some sort o' firework, with a fuse that'd burn for some time before it went off, then there wasn't any doubt who the killer was. We didn't think of Brockwell at first because 'e seemed ter be in danger 'imself an' ter 'ave no motive . . . '

'All that playing-card rubbish to direct our attention to Naylor,' said the Chief Constable; 'it was a pretty clever idea . . . '

'When I first read about this case,' remarked Mr. Budd, 'I said it was a lot o' story-book hokum, an' that's just what it was. When people commit murders they don't bother about leavin' cards, or flowers, or any such nonsense. I was always suspicious o' *that* . . . '

'You're quite right, of course,' agreed Major Toppington. 'Why in the world do you suppose that girl — Sandra — wanted Custer to deliver that note?'

'Well, it's my opinion, sir,' replied Mr. Budd, 'that Brockwell was behind that note. I think 'e gave it to 'er to give to Custer an' pitched 'er some yarn to account fer it. o' course, 'is *real* reason was ter ram 'ome to us about the royal flush. 'e was afraid we might miss the point . . . '

'I suppose,' said the Chief Constable, musingly, 'that that was the beginning of it all. When Brockwell found that George Naylor's son was living in the district, I mean?'

'Yes, I think so, sir,' said the big man. 'I believe it was because o' that that he persuaded 'is wife to come 'ere an' build this 'ouse. Maybe it was because of Harriet Lake, too. Anyway, I think that's what started the whole idea in his mind — the scheme for all these murders, an' the playing-cards . . . '

'The poison in the brandy was a good touch,' said Major Toppington.

'An' so was the marks in the cupboard,' said Mr. Budd. ''e made 'em 'imself, of course . . . '

'The man's a good actor,' said the Chief Constable. 'All that display of fear was very well done, you know.'

'Only it wasn't actin',' said Mr. Budd. ''e *was* scared — scared that we'd find out the truth. We thought that 'e was afraid o' the murderer, that's all.' He took a cigar from his pocket, sniffed it, and bit off the end. ''e wasn't really clever,' he went on. 'I scared 'im a lot when I suggested 'e should send for his lawyer an' make a new will. 'e couldn't do that without the source o' the money comin' out.' He produced a box of matches, struck a match and lit his cigar, a proceeding which the Chief Constable viewed with alarm. He had smelt one of Mr. Budd's atrocious cigars before.

'Well, whether he ever comes up for trial or not,' he remarked, thankfully, 'the case is over, and I'm very glad. It gave me more worry and anxiety than I've had for years.'

'Me, too, sir,' said Mr. Budd, blowing out a cloud of poisonous smoke, which resulted in Major Toppington hastily inventing an excuse and taking his leave.

5

Henry Brockwell died during the night, without recovering consciousness. A further hæmorrhage of the brain resulted in convulsions and finally death.

'He had an abnormally high blood pressure which the amount of drink he consumed didn't help,' said Doctor Middlesham, who was with him till the last. 'Shock did the rest . . . '

Mr. Budd felt relieved when he heard the news. It was going to save him, and a lot of other people, a great deal of hard work in preparing a case for a jury.

'Well,' he said, after breakfast, going into the kitchen. 'There's nuthin' ter stop yer going now, Custer, when yer want to, an' that applies to you, ma'am.'

'H'I shall leave this h'afternoon,' declared Mrs. Bleecher. 'H'and glad enough I shall be to go. When I think that I might 'ave bin murdered in me bed at h'any minute. I'm sure I oughter be thankful that I'm still alive . . . '

'An' don' you go thinking of alterin' any more cheques,' said Mr. Budd to Tommy Custer, later. 'If you've got any sense you'll find another job . . . '

'I've already got one,' said Tommy Custer, cheerfully. 'I'm goin' ter work fer Miss Lake an' Mr. Naylor . . . '

'What, both of 'em?' said Mr. Budd.

'Same thing as one,' answered Mr. Custer, with a wink. 'They're gettin' spliced next month . . . '

'Cousins, h'm.' The big man shook his head doubtfully. 'Oh, well, I s'pose they know what they're doin' . . . '

'You bet yer life they does,' declared Tommy Custer.

'Well, don' you go runnin' off with the weddin' presents,' warned Mr. Budd, 'or you'll 'ave me comin' after yer double quick.'

'You couldn't tempt me ter go crooked with a bushel o' quid notes,' said Mr. Custer. 'All that belongs ter me past . . . '

'See that it don't get mixed up with yer future,' said Mr. Budd, and he walked away.

For his own satisfaction, and to clear up a point which had puzzled him, he paid a visit to Brockwell's bank and saw the manager. The account was practically nil. There had never been a large balance for more than a few days. When one of the cheques, which Harriet Lake had mentioned, had been presented, just sufficient cash had been deposited to meet it on the previous day. This came from Mrs. Brockwell's account in a London bank. She had allowed Brockwell to sign cheques for an account which, normally, held only a pound or two. It was a very good thing for them, thought Mr. Budd, that Harriet Lake and Tommy Custer's scheme had never been put into practice. They would have had an unpleasant shock.

He called at the cottage in Mill Lane on his way back, and Harriet opened the door.

'You again?' she said, smiling.

'Me again,' agreed Mr. Budd. 'An' for the last time. It's all over an' I'm goin' back ter town this afternoon . . .'

'Do you mean you've caught the murderer . . . ?' she gasped. 'Come in and tell me all about it . . . '

Mr. Budd went in and told her all about it.

'I'm not surprised,' she said. 'Brockwell was capable of anything, though I never suspected him of this . . . '

'No more did I, miss,' said Mr. Budd. 'Not until I found the motive 'e 'ad . . . I 'ear you're gettin' married?'

'Who told you — Custer?' she demanded, and he nodded.

'Nice feller, Mr. Naylor,' he remarked. 'That feller who's been followin' 'im about'll come an' guard the weddin' presents if you ask 'im . . . '

'No, thank you,' she said, firmly. 'I don't want to see any more detectives for the rest of my life.'

'Thank you, miss,' murmured Mr. Budd.

'Oh, I don't mean *you*,' she amended, hastily. 'You're not a detective . . . '

'You don't know 'ow nearly right you are, miss,' said Mr. Budd, as she began to stammer an apology.

'I didn't mean it *that* way,' she said.

'There's one thing I would like ter know,' he said, after a pause. 'It's just a

369

matter o' personal curiosity, an' 'asn't got anythin' ter do with the case. Why did your father let Brockwell swindle 'im outer that three thousand pounds?'

She frowned and hesitated.

'You don't 'ave ter tell me if you don't want to,' he said. 'Maybe I'm bein' nosy, an' should mind me own business . . . '

'I'll tell you,' she said, suddenly. 'At least I'll tell you partly . . . It was blackmail . . . Brockwell blackmailed my father into parting with the money . . . I'm *not* going to tell you how . . . '

'That's all right, miss,' said Mr. Budd. 'Thank you fer tellin' me anything . . . '

He said good-bye to her and drove slowly back to The Croft. On the way he saw Joshua Craven in the High Street. The reporter called to him and, against his inclination, he stopped the car.

'I hear that Brockwell's dead?' said Mr. Craven, abruptly. 'A very sudden demise from all accounts. Dear me, it's a great pity — a very great pity. However, it will, no doubt, save the hangman a job . . . '

'You believed 'e was guilty?' said Mr. Budd, in genuine surprise.

'From the first, my dear sir, from the first,' answered Mr. Craven. 'The motive was so plain, don't you think . . . ?'

'Did you know that the money was 'is wife's?' demanded the big man.

'Of course.' Mr. Craven regarded him with a pitying smile. 'I'm afraid I tried to lead you away from the truth so that I should have time to complete my case, but you got in first after all. Red herrings, my dear sir, red herrings, that's all. By the way, *re* Edward Lake. Brockwell blackmailed him out of that three thousand pounds . . . '

'I know that,' snapped Mr. Budd, a little irritably.

'Do you, indeed?' said Mr. Craven. 'Well, well. Yes, Edward Lake committed bigamy. His first wife was alive when he married his second. In justice to his memory he did it unknowingly, but it is rather unfortunate for his daughter, who was a child of the — er — second union.'

So that was why Harriet Lake had only told him part of the truth, thought Mr. Budd. Well, he couldn't altogether blame her . . .

'I must be going,' said Joshua Craven. 'I have my article to write. I think it will prove interesting reading. Ah, there goes Miss Pipp-Partington . . . What a charming girl. Our doctor friend is a very lucky man, don't you think? I'm afraid she dislikes me. I got her to admit, quite unintentionally on her part, that she had a brother . . . Well, good-bye, my dear sir. I hope we shall meet again soon.'

He waved his hand and walked on, leaving Mr. Budd with a sincere wish that his hope would not be gratified. A little of Mr. Craven went a very long way indeed.

When he reached The Croft he found Leek already packed and waiting.

'Thought you was never comin',' complained the sergeant. 'Where 'ave you bin?'

'Just tyin' up a few loose ends,' said Mr. Budd.

'It's a good thing it's all over,' said Leek. 'I was gettin' fed-up with it . . .'

'Were yer now?' remarked Mr. Budd. 'Well, considerin' that you've spent most o' the time asleep, I don't see 'ow yer could . . .'

'Asleep?' echoed Leek. 'Well, I like that . . . '

'I know yer do,' broke in Mr. Budd, 'but you can't live in a perpetual state of coma. Come an' help me pack.'

He went up the stairs to his room, followed by the reluctant sergeant.

'You was lucky to pull this off, yer know,' said Leek, with great satisfaction. 'You was wrong right up ter the last, wasn't yer?'

'I'm like Great Britain,' answered Mr. Budd, complacently. 'I lose all the battles *except* the last one . . . '

THE END

We do hope that you have enjoyed reading this large print book.

Did you know that all of our titles are available for purchase?

We publish a wide range of high quality large print books including:
Romances, Mysteries, Classics
General Fiction
Non Fiction and Westerns

Special interest titles available in large print are:
The Little Oxford Dictionary
Music Book, Song Book
Hymn Book, Service Book

Also available from us courtesy of Oxford University Press:
Young Readers' Dictionary
(large print edition)
Young Readers' Thesaurus
(large print edition)

For further information or a free brochure, please contact us at:
Ulverscroft Large Print Books Ltd.,
The Green, Bradgate Road, Anstey,
Leicester, LE7 7FU, England.
Tel: (00 44) 0116 236 4325
Fax: (00 44) 0116 234 0205

MYSTERY IN MOON LANE

A. A. Glynn

What could be the explanation for that strange affair of the corpse in old-fashioned clothing, taken from a burning building in Moon Lane by rescuers during the Blitz, Christmas 1940? Who is the mysterious young woman who models for young artist Jevons as he paints in a haze? What is the myth of the seal woman, and should Dan and his wife Leonora be afraid? Ghosts, myths and ancient curses are the subjects of six stories from the pen of A.A. Glynn.

THE CAPTIVE CLAIRVOYANT

Brian Ball

The Baker Street Irregulars, the gang of ragamuffins who sometimes assist Sherlock Holmes in his investigations, put their wits and courage to the test against kidnapping, robbery and murder . . . A boy announces that he has seen a ghost, but the truth is far more terrifying . . . A gypsy seeks vengeance from beyond the grave . . . An ancient evil awakens and desires fresh victims . . . These five stories of mystery, horror and the occult from the pen of Brian Ball will thrill and chill in equal measure.